BRIDES OF BLESSINGS

Love More Precious Than Gold

BEAUTY BEYOND UNDERSTANDING

BEAUTY BEYOND UNDERSTANDING

BRIDES OF BLESSINGS: BOOK 10

KARI TRUMBO

"*Adventure, travel and finding the truth make for a very interesting read with a few twists and turns and the answers found in Blessings.*" ∼ Amazon Reviewer

"*Bounty Beyond Reason is my first Kari Trumbo novel, but it most definitely will not be my last. This book is FANTASTIC! It has so much action and passion that I could not put the book down. When I had to, I did it begrudgingly! This story is so engaging, the characters are well written, and the romance is perfect. The villains are quite awful, and when justice is served I was left quite satisfied.*" ∼ Nicole S. Amazon Reviewer

"*I absolutely enjoyed every moment spent in the pages of this story. The characters are vivid and real. The story setting is depicted with such detail, that you feel like you are there in the forest, walking on the trails, smelling the loamy earth after a rain. I enjoyed the adventure and the mystery. I often couldn't turn the pages fast enough to find out what would happen next. I was loathed to put the book down for even a moment."* ~ Amazon Reviewer

"Bounty Beyond Reason is a well written tale with just the right blend of drama and romance with a bit of suspense thrown in for good measure. The message of forgiveness and redemption is strong but is woven into the story nicely. This is one book that lovers of western romance should not miss." ~ Amazon Reviewer

April rains pattered against the front window of the mercantile as Lenora Abernathy stood listening to the owner, Ed Mosier, tell everyone a long story about his uncle. The Mosiers owned another store somewhere far off, a distant place she'd never heard of. It was such a long-past, sweet memory to live where goods were easy to come by and where female companionship was plentiful. Here, in Blessings, nothing was abundant except heat in the summer and rain in the spring, not even the women. She was friends with just about every woman who called the small mining town home, but it would make for a scant party. If she invited every one of them, she still wouldn't have enough guests to fill her house, though one wouldn't come. Seraphina. Because Lenora's husband would never allow the *witch* into his home.

Whit, from Pullen Freight, came in hefting a huge

sack marked, "Postal Carrier". "Mail call!" he yelled, laughing as Ed gave him a stern look.

"I'm supposed to say that." He shook his finger at Whit, but his lined forehead melted into a smile a moment later.

He reached in and pulled out a handful of mail. A crumpled, thin white envelope lay on top. It looked like it had seen the whole world and then some. Ed picked up the battered note and squinted at the crumpled pencil marks. His eyes went wide and the color drained from his face as he slowly handed the envelope to her and blinked, his mouth hanging slightly agape.

"It's for you, and your pa." His hand trembled as he held it out to her and suddenly all the joy whooshed from the room. All the light conversation stopped and the people standing about turned to stare with open interest.

Who would write to her? Whose name on the return address would bother Ed so? She reached out and took the letter, wishing her husband, Victor, could be there with her. He was at the livery, making a living for them and their growing child. She rubbed her belly absentmindedly as she focused on the letter.

Her gut twisted at the handwriting and her skin turned from cold to red hot.

"Who is it?" Atherton's kind old eyes appeared before her and he gripped her arm. She'd forgotten the mercantile was well-populated at that time of day and she might make a spectacle of herself.

"It's Geoff." She took two steps back, taking in all the worried faces around her. "I need to go find Father."

CHAPTER 1

Outside Blessings, California
May 1856

If Geoff walked parallel to the trail, leading his horse with no name, no one would see him and hopefully wouldn't hear either. It had been so long since he'd been there, and life hadn't been easy in the meantime, so it was difficult to remember just where Blessings was.

He kept an eye out for both bear and man. If he remembered correctly, the Miwak camp was nearby and he didn't need to start anything in the dead of night. Nor did he want anyone from Blessings to know he was back. Yet. His plan had seemed foolproof when he'd made it a month before. He'd sent a letter to warn his father and sister Lenora he would be on his way. Then he'd given them time to get accustomed to the idea of his return. Finally, tonight, he'd show up when they thought he'd forgotten. That way he could explain, or at least try, before they kicked him out on his rear.

An owl hooted at him from above and twigs snapped beneath his boots—he and his newly gangly frame were sorely out of his element. He'd left Blessings at the age of seventeen, not yet full-grown. Now, at over twenty, he'd finally quit growing. Geoff Farnsworth had no business wandering through the woods in the dead of night, especially if he meant to keep his presence hidden. The only other time he'd bothered had been when he'd arrived in California five years before. He and his family, along with two men hired to protect them, had traveled from the bay of San Francisco to Blessings. He'd hated every minute of it.

Gambling was his new profession. He'd been nothing but a gambler and wastrel almost since he'd wandered away from Blessings with no plan to return. It had kept him fed and clothed, so he'd considered himself pretty good at it. When he'd allowed himself to get sober, however, he remembered that he'd left his family to deal with the loss of *Maman*. Because he'd been too much of a spoiled child to deal with it. He hadn't been able to face his father and admit he had no desire to be a lawyer and follow in his footsteps. Instead, he'd chosen to dishonor his father and walk away from his family. He still didn't want to face them because his father wasn't getting any younger. *Maman* had been buried since just days after he'd left, but her memory still haunted him. He'd finally succumbed to the fact that he had to return, or go crazy just like she had.

A shadow slithered by from the corner of his eye and he yanked his horse to a stop beside him. Cold fear wrapped around his neck and choked his words. "Who goes there?" Blast the trees and the darkness. He couldn't see anything, and couldn't risk a lantern even if he had one. It could've been a deer, or a man. He'd only caught the hint of movement.

He swung his head in search of whatever had moved and his horse, a dappled beauty he'd won in his last game, stomped the twigs and grass stubble underfoot. He could've taken the road into Blessings, but if he had, someone might have noticed him. They certainly would've noticed the horse. Blessings never really slept, it had always had a certain night life, so someone would've been about. The saloon had been one of the first buildings built, so the men were used to it. It had been there even before Geoff and his family had come, and they had been some of the first to Blessings.

Nothing else moved along the path, no matter how he squinted and searched. The horse blew great puffs from his flared nostrils. "Easy, boy," he whispered, holding tight to the halter and hoping whatever it was would just move along. Whatever had moved, it seemed as hesitant to make itself known as he was to keep going. Could it be waiting for him to move so it could pounce?

He tugged the horse's halter and directed it along between the evergreens, the pungent scent filling the air. The silence all around crept up his spine, and every brush of dried pine needles against his boots was like the crackle of a campfire. He kept watch from the corner of his eye to the spot where he'd seen movement. Just when he was about out of range of sight, something moved again and he stopped, whipping around to check the trees again. If only he'd been able to win back his gun. The horse was a good thing to own, but the gun would've been a sight more useful against a mountain lion or bear.

"I know you're there. Come out." He waited, praying he wasn't speaking to an animal that would jump out and try to make a meal of him. His father wouldn't even know to look for him. His plan was falling apart the closer he got to Blessings. With his heart racing, he stared into the shadowy depths of the trees.

The horse shuffled again, nerves coursing through his strong, corded neck. It didn't like being out there in the darkness without a trail any more than he did. It was possible the horse was reacting to his own tension and Geoff tried to make himself relax, but that just served to make the horse tug harder to try to get away.

"You can't leave, boy. I'm of no mind to be out here alone."

A woman slowly inched out from behind a tree. Her red, hooded cape obscured her face, but her size, grace and bell-shaped silhouette bespoke of a woman. The horse tugged on his hold and pulled free. Geoff swiped at the reins before the animal could bolt.

"*Beinvenue aux Blessings.*" She slid her hood down to her shoulders with hands like pearls in the moonlight. A flower adorned her ear on her right side, and she seemed to almost glow after the darkness of her cape. She was as beautiful as he imagined an angel to be, and with the way her skin seemed to reflect the scant moonlight, she almost glowed like he imagined an angel would.

"So, I'm close? I couldn't remember. Thank you for the welcome." He touched his hat, then yanked his hand away. The middle of the forest at night was no place for pleasantries. After all the fearsome things he'd conjured in his head meeting him in the forest, this woman was like a breath of cool air. He held out his hand and she stepped away from him, her eyes staring from his outstretched fingers up to his face and back again. So distrustful. Perhaps she really was an angel, sent to guide him? "I won't hurt you." He took a step closer.

She lingered, though the quiver of her fingers as she tugged her cape back in place made him step back again. He took that moment to regain his hold on the horse's halter. If he lost the horse, he'd lose the one thing he had of value.

He touched his chest. "Geoff Farnsworth."

The woman gasped, then smiled. "Lenora?" Her fear seemed to melt away and she approached with a few slow steps.

The horse blasted her a warning to stay back and he held tight to the reins. "Your name is Lenora?" All of a sudden he couldn't remember a single one of those French lessons his mother had forced him to sit through. "*Vous...?*" He clenched his eyes shut trying to remember, but it was so long ago. "No, that's not right. *Votre nom?*" His mother would've slapped his hands with a ruler for such a poor attempt.

The woman smiled slightly and laid a delicate hand

7

to her chest. She looked him in the eye and in her soft French accent, she said, "I am Seraphina Beaumont."

Her voice enchanted him, soft, melodic. He wanted to see her face again. His horse took that moment to yank his head down, loosing the halter from his grip. He took off right for Miss Beaumont, and she screamed, covering her face with one arm, as the horse mowed her over and kept running.

"No! Blasted horse, come back!" He should've named the stupid beast. He rushed over to where Seraphina lay in the grass. She groaned softly as he touched the shoulder that had taken a direct hit.

"Are you all right?" He couldn't see her eyes in the darkness at the base of the trees. He unbuttoned her cape to see if she had any injuries and found she wore a black mourning gown under the red cape, making it impossible to tell if she had further injuries or not. He couldn't see a thing in the dark.

"Home," she rasped, and pointed to a spot through the trees.

"Can you stand, if I help you?" Meeting her in the woods was such an odd circumstance. He wasn't even sure what to do. She grasped his hand and tried to pull herself up, but her gasp cut through the night. He prayed she didn't live far and that whomever she lived with could help her. When he'd left, Blessings didn't even have a doctor, just a witch that lived in the woods near Cort and Victor's gambling tent. One who only came out at night and wore a red cape. The realization shocked every part of him and he almost dropped her as he stood.

"Wait," he said, trying to find her face in the pool of darkness under her hood. "You're the witch."

THE HUGE HORSE had knocked Seraphina back, landing hard on her shoulder, then stepped on her wrist as it had trotted off. The motion was so quick, she'd been too shocked to move. Then the pain came and she couldn't catch her breath. Lenora's brother, Geoff, the one Lenora had complained about for years, had returned. Meeting someone in the dead of night who was both stranger and not, left her unsure of how to act or even proceed. If she were a true friend, she would trust what Lenora had said about Geoff, yet he hadn't been threatening in the slightest.

Seraphina tried to push herself off the ground, but her shoulder wouldn't hold her weight and her wrist throbbed for attention. In a moment, she found herself in the arms of the brother of her dearest friend. Her heart raced, making her wrist throb. Once she was close enough to see him, though it was dark, she knew he couldn't be much older than her own twenty-two years. His arms didn't falter in the slightest and he mumbled something at her as he lifted her closer, then his arms seemed to slacken and she gasped as he lost his hold for a moment.

"You're the witch." He froze in his place and she braced herself to be dropped. Her uninjured arm was held between her own body and his, so she couldn't hold tight to him to prevent it.

She wasn't really a witch, never had been. But people seemed rather set in their ways, not only in Blessings but everywhere she and her brother had landed. Her brother, Martin, had finally tired of her three years before. He'd simply left for work one morning and never returned. She couldn't go to the sheriff—it wasn't as if she could just walk around in the daylight—and no one had ever come to check for him. Either they didn't care about his absence, had known he was leaving, or were too frightened of her to come ask. No matter, she had no idea where he'd gone and he obviously wasn't going to return.

"Non." She stopped, then forced herself to use the English Lenora had been teaching her for four years, though it was difficult. "Not a witch."

He stood, staring at her for a full minute, then shook his head and sighed before he seemed to make up his mind and strode toward her cabin. At least he seemed to remember where her little homestead was. He'd visited the gambling tent that had been near her home enough when he'd first been in Blessings to know, at least that's what Lenora had said. Seraphina's brother's disappearance had given Lenora ample chance to tell her all about Geoff and his shortcomings, thinking Seraphina would make a willing audience.

He glanced down at her as he stopped by her door. "Do I need to knock? Is someone waiting for you inside?" Only when he spoke did she hear his strain.

She shook her head and he shoved the door open.

There were no lamps lit inside, but she'd pulled back all the curtains she normally left over the windows during the day. Light made her skin burn and bubble, so she couldn't be in the sunlight. She'd tried every herb and tincture she could make, had spoken with the Miwok across the river about their medicine, had asked every doctor she and her brother had met along the way from France to California, but no one could help her. So she never went out in the day, and everyone assumed she was a witch. How else to explain such a creature of the night?

He laid her on the bed in the corner and swiped a shaking hand down his face. "I don't know what I should do. I feel horrible, but I must go find my horse, without it, I can't keep going. I also have to talk to my family, they don't even know I'm coming, but I hate to just leave you." His voice droned, low and steady.

"Go." She could manage on her own. She always had. Her body was strong enough to heal. After a day of rest, she would be back up again and working. "Just please, close the curtains before you go." If he didn't and she couldn't get up to do it, even the indirect sun from the windows might do damage. She'd been so careful for so long, she wasn't certain how close she needed to get to the light to be burned. The burns were incredibly painful and she didn't want to take the chance.

He cocked his head as he moved to the window at the end of her bed and untied the thick cord she used to hold it at night. Once that fell, he did likewise with the one other window in the small cabin. Once he finished, he turned to her and his mouth slackened, a question forming under the soft ripple in his forehead.

"I don't understand, but I did as you asked." Then he touched his hat and left, closing the door softly behind him.

If only the world held more people like the Farnsworths, who just did what was right and didn't listen to others. After his footfalls were far away, Seraphina gently ran her fingers over her wrist. The pain was so intense tears sprang to her eyes. She couldn't be sure if it was broken or not, but it swelled quickly.

She lay on her blanket to hold it down, then tore a long edge from her sheet. Though the room was dark, she could feel no protrusion through her skin. As she wrapped her wrist, she had to stop, letting the waves of darkness pass as the pain would peak, then subside. Once the task was done, she lay back in her bed, a cold sweat covering her.

Geoff was the first person to visit her cabin since his sister had abandoned her months before. Right after learning of her pregnancy, Lenora had stopped coming. Seraphina had even made a gift for Lenora, a small bottle of oil of castor, in case her time should come but the baby wasn't ready, and dried red raspberry leaves to aid her in pain relief after the birth. But Lenora hadn't come and, after a few weeks, Seraphina had put the items back on her wall for another mother. If one ever came.

She would need to rest and heal. No one was going to help her find food and do what she needed to do daily to survive. Broken wrist or not, she had to push on.

CHAPTER 2

Geoff made his way from the witch's cabin slowly toward Blessings. Though he was still in the woods, there had been much more clearing done than the last time Geoff had been in Blessings. Now, trees were scattered loosely, revealing other homesteads that hadn't been there before. The place where the gaming tent had once been was now a small cabin with a lean-to off the back. All the windows were dark. He could still feel the heat from a recently snuffed fire and a ribbon of smoke curled to the sky. If he had to guess by the moon, it was perhaps near ten and many would be abed. A woman sang a lullaby softly within as he made his way past.

There was little chance he would find his horse in Blessings, or ever again. It didn't know him, nor did it have a name for him to claim it. If anyone found it, the horse would be just as much theirs as his. Now he truly had nothing but the clothes on his back. He hadn't even packed a bag because he had nothing to bring.

On the edge of the town proper, he glanced over the sprawling, slightly sloped area. When he'd left, there had been the bar, the gaming tent, his father's law office, the mercantile with the mine office, and a tiny church. Now, there were businesses all up and down the street, not that he could read any of their names from where he stood. When he'd left, Victor, the man who'd tried to woo his sister, had come after him and found him gambling in nearby Coloma. Victor had told him to come back, but he'd needed his time and he'd cursed Victor for trying, especially since Victor was a gambler himself. Geoff wouldn't have done anyone any good then. Since he hadn't returned with Victor, his father had probably been alone all this time, unless he lived with Lenora. If he did, he would find neither of them until later.

He trudged toward the street, listening to the tinny piano as it jangled from the bar. It mingled with the stomping and whoops of men clapping along. A woman sang, but he didn't pay any heed to the words. He'd heard them all before. On the corner, just as he'd left it, stood his father's land and law office. A lump formed in his throat as he scanned the two-story building. The day after he'd left, his mother had jumped to her death off that building. Ever since he'd found out, his mother had haunted him, begging him to come back. Now he was.

"Is this what you wanted, *Maman*?" he rasped as he scanned the high roof line as if some part of her still remained. But her ghost was, for once, silent.

He trudged up the stairs of the side entrance to his father's home and knocked lightly on the door. In the past, his father had always been one to stay up late and read, and he hoped that the habit remained. Inside, someone slowly came to the door and a moment later, his father pulled it open slightly, first his shock of white hair then his cool blue eyes peered around.

"Geoff? Is that really you?" He pulled the door open a little more, his open-eyed shock a surprise. Hadn't he received the letter?

"Yes, I'm back. That is, if you'll have me." His father tugged him inside and before he could even look around, he found himself in a crushing embrace. His father had never been warm, had never shown much affection to either him or Lenora, and Geoff was unsure of how to react, save for wanting to get away.

"Of course, how long will you be staying?" He pulled away from Geoff and held his shoulders, staring over his face. His father's open interest was more than Geoff had expected, and almost uncomfortable after living without people for so long. His skin itched to throw off his father's touch and return to the solitude, but he couldn't. He had to know about his past.

"I don't know, Father. I'd planned to see you, see how you and Lenora were faring. Then, I'll decide what to do with my life." Though he wanted to tell his father right there that he wanted nothing to do with being a lawyer, that it wasn't in his blood, the hour was late. If his father had not shunned him as he'd thought, then there was no reason to fight after he'd just arrived. He turned to look around the space that had been his father's home for half a decade. It didn't look at all like it had when he'd left.

"I had to change some things. There were to many reminders," his father offered absently.

Geoff nodded to let him know that he didn't have to explain further. He wished he could do some rearranging of his own to get his mother out of his thoughts and dreams. Maybe now that he'd finally come back, she would. He'd rearranged his whole life to achieve it.

"Lenora has been married now for four years," his father said, then turned to the sitting room and motioned for him to sit.

Lenora was the one he needed to see most of all, because he was still so unsure how his father would react to knowing he wouldn't take over the business. She had more of a connection to *Maman*, and might be able to answer his questions. She was the key to what he needed to know. "And just how is she getting on?"

It was late, well past the time to retire for most of respectable society, yet here he was with his father, sitting down to chat as if nothing stood between them, but the time lost was thicker than a wall. He moved into the sitting room and chose a chair in the corner.

He mumbled something and Geoff moved to change the subject. "You've had a lot of furniture delivered. When I left, you didn't even have beds yet." They had slept on wooden pallets with as many blankets as they could gather to soften them. He'd grown up with a feather bed his whole life until that point and the indignity of the whole trip had changed him. In some

16

ways, he agreed with his mother completely—they never should've left Boston.

"Yes, well, I've had a long time to acquire it." His father took a chair near the fire. The extra glow lit his face and Geoff noticed how old his father had become in the space of time he'd been gone. Lines of age had marked his eyes, his nose seemed bigger on his face and his chin seemed to hang where it had been firm before.

"I'm sorry, Father. I know you needed me, but I had to go off on my own. It was selfish, but I didn't belong in Blessings. I'm still not sure I belong here, but I needed to see you. I needed to know that you and Lenora were all right. You're all I have. I feel this need to be near family, to know all I can about who I am. Mother's side has never wanted anything to do with us, and I don't expect they ever will."

Father cast his gaze into his lap. "I expect not."

There was a pull though, to reach out for something he'd lost and he prayed it was more than for a mother he would never see again. He needed to feel connected to someone. He missed his father and Lenora, and his mother.

"You're welcome in Blessings as long as you want to stay, but Lenora, she's still angry. You weren't here. She was up on the roof with your mother when she jumped. She won't talk about it, never has, left everyone to think she wasn't affected by it, but all that hurt came out as anger against you. That's what you'll be fighting against."

He owed his sister that much. He'd taken her dream of being a lawyer and tossed it aside as if it were nothing, and then he'd run off, leaving her to deal with not only the pain of loss, but of a grieving father as well.

"I only hope she can forgive me before I move on. If I can't find what I seek here, I'll find Mother's family, somehow. I won't stay if she doesn't want me here, and frankly, there's no reason to stay if she doesn't."

Father glanced up at him, his eyes tired and worn. "So be it." He stood and pulled his house robe tightly about him, then went over to a small lap desk his mother had brought to Blessings in their trunk. He opened it and pulled out a small black book. "This was your mother's. Lenora doesn't know about it, but if you feel you need to move on, this book will at least give you a destination. I don't have anywhere for you to sleep here, I'm afraid. There is a boarding house and they always have room. If I was sure Lenora would have you, I'd just send you over there, but it's not a good time to test her."

Geoff nodded and held in a yawn. He'd spent more time helping Seraphina than he'd intended and it was later than he'd planned to arrive. Seeing Lenora would be impossible this late, even if he had been welcome. "I'm sure I'll get to see her soon enough. In the meantime, I'm going to go check in with some old friends. I'll see you in the morning, Father." While he did have a few old acquaintances who were still in town, Victor and Cort, he'd been thinking of a much newer friend. One who probably actually needed his attendance. He slid his hat back on his head and closed the door behind him.

THOUGH SHE NORMALLY WOKE AT dusk and took to her bed at dawn, the pain of her injuries kept Seraphina in bed and she'd slept through the night as a normal person would. Waking after a sleep at such an odd time for her left her feeling out of sorts, though there was something else amiss. Her skin prickled as she sensed her world through closed eyes, the layers of sleep shifting around her thoughts.

The prickle turned to a burn and her eyes flew open with the realization of what was happening. The window covers that had been closed when she'd fallen asleep were pulled wide letting in the morning sun. The only two people who would willingly come into her home, her brother and Lenora, would never open the covers. The burning in her skin intensified until it felt like scalding water. She used the headboard to pull herself up and untied the cord, letting the curtain fall closed.

Who would do such a thing? Not that anyone but those who were close to her knew of her malady. No one would understand how it hurt her. Even now, she could feel the intense heat on her skin, but the sunlight hadn't touched her, it would cool soon.

"Heaven's mercy." Geoff's voice cut through her thoughts and she swung her head to face him, but couldn't scream. His eyes grew wide as he stared at her wrist. Convincing him she was not a witch would be even harder now. Most likely her face was covered with bumps and burns that appeared on her skin like magic when she was exposed to the light.

"What are you doing here?" Her native French came

easily as she covered her cheeks with her hands, hoping he wouldn't see just how badly the sun could damage her, but she found her cheeks still clear.

He'd been laying on her floor, and now knelt by her bed. "I felt pretty bad for what happened last night. I talked to my father, then came back here to check on you. I opened the curtain to let in some moonlight to help me see, but even in sleep you wouldn't let me near enough to take a look at it." He laughed and scratched the back of his neck, either out of nerves or discomfort after sleeping on the floor, she couldn't tell which.

She rubbed her shoulder and though she was sure, even without looking, that it was a bit swollen and most likely bruised, it wasn't broken. Her wrist was another matter. That still hurt even when she breathed. "I'm sure I'll be fine. You need not worry about me." She settled herself back on her bed.

At her parents' small flat back in France, homeless men and women had often come and shared the thin soup *Maman* served to any who stopped by. They would stay and curl up to sleep on any open space on the floor. Waking to a stranger laying on her floor was not unheard of, but this stranger left far more questions than comfort on her mind.

"What can I do?" he reached up and pulled her hand away from her face, and stared at the bandage. "Did my horse do that? Last night? It was so dark, I don't remember if your wrist was wrapped or not. I saw him hit you—"

His eyes softened but she pulled away, tugging her

20

blanket up to cover her nose and face. How could he worry about her wrist when she had to be covered in blisters? She always did when her skin prickled like that. He stood and strode to the other side of the cabin, pulling the cord on the curtain. A moment later, the room fell into blessed darkness. She'd never been one to love the light, preferring the coolness of the shadows. But there was a certain unease about being in the darkened room with a man she only knew of second-hand.

Geoff struck a match and swung it around, located her lamp on the table and lit it, then turned back to her. "There. Now that the room is the way you asked me to leave it, can we talk now? Or will you hide? Maybe you know less English than I think? I can try French. I might remember a little." He rubbed his hands down the front of his trousers and mumbled, "It would be easier to go find my horse with nothing more than my nose than to remember classes from so long ago."

If he was anything like his sister, he would know some, but not much. Lenora had tried her best to converse with Seraphina way back when the family had first arrived in Blessings. Seraphina knew some English, more since knowing Lenora, but still found her speech faltering.

"I speak some English," she mumbled from under the blanket. More than speaking, she wanted him to go away. Though she'd never seen in a mirror what the sun did to her face, she had felt it. The bumps would fill with liquid soon and they would itch. She needed to get salve on them quickly, but that wasn't something she could do with this man just standing there. She gingerly reached for her cheeks once more, but found nothing, which was puzzling.

"I can manage on my own. I have for years." She waited, hoping he would admit defeat, collect himself, and go so she could make her way to her wall of tinctures and get the remedy she needed.

"Well, if it's all the same, I'd like to stick around and make sure. It was my horse that knocked you over, and honestly, you're about the only reason I'm staying in Blessings. At least for now. I'd wanted to see my sister, but my father tells me that might not be such a good idea for a while."

With as angry as Lenora was about her brother, it could put her pregnancy in danger. "She is," Seraphina searched for the long word Lenora had used when speaking of her condition, "del-i-cate right now."

Geoff laughed and pretended to look at all her medicines and tinctures as he gently touched a few of the bottles. Most of the glass bottles were from whiskey and other libations, she'd merely dug through the refuse piles behind various Blessings homes and the bar and saved them.

"Delicate? That isn't what my father said. I think he said she was furious. They are equally strong words, but mean something totally different."

She shook her head and laughed at his attempt to teach her English. "I know she is furious, I was talking about her state. She shouldn't get angry right now. It isn't healthy."

He turned and the moment her words made sense his mouth dropped open. "Are you saying what I think you're saying?"

"I don't understand your meaning." Some things in English made no sense. Of course she was saying what she said, why else would she say it?

"A baby," the words seemed to trail off his tongue. Geoff's eyes roamed the room, but saw nothing. "Family."

Since he didn't seem at all ready to leave, Seraphina pushed with her good arm to get up out of bed and went over to her shelves of medicinals, shuffling him out of the way slightly, and pulling down one particular amber bottle. She knew them all by memory. Once she'd opened the cork, she poured a small amount of the contents on her hand. It was green and oily, but helped with the burn. After gently rubbing it on her face, and keeping herself turned from her guest, the sting began to subside.

"Well, that changes everything. Since you know so much about my sister, can you help me find a way to see her without making her furious?"

The man had been nothing but trouble since she'd followed him into Blessings to make sure he made it without incident. Now, he wanted more help from her. She felt the admonishment of the Holy Spirit even before she finished the thought. She'd prayed for the Lord to rid her of her loneliness. Years of prayers. Now someone had finally come who wasn't terrified of her, she couldn't send him away.

"Lenora is my only friend in all of Blessings. A few

are kind, but none see me as Lenora does. I won't hurt her."

He stepped closer and a half-smile warmed his eyes. "I don't want you to hurt her. I merely want to bring this family back together. It's a noble goal, not a false one."

Though the words should have healed her wounded heart, they only tore it further. Together was a word she would never again experience without her brother and with the distrust of everyone she met. "Then you have my word." She reached out her hand without thinking, then pulled it away. Though her hands had taken in less of the direct light, she could see small bumps all along the back and between her fingers. He reached for it anyway and gave it a gentle shake. No man had ever asked for her word, nor would they have taken the word of a witch. This man—whom her closest friend had labeled a horrible beast—was the first person to ever give her that respect, and the first to willingly touch her after a burn. She glanced at her hand then up to his warm brown eyes.

"Good, that means you're stuck with me for a little while."

CHAPTER 3

The tiny cabin offered little in the way of escape, nor did it offer much to talk about. Seraphina stood next to her bed, consternation marring the waxy delicate sheen of her skin. In the moonlight, she'd almost seemed to glow, but in the diffused light of day, she appeared to have almost a sickly pallor that made him even more concerned for her health. While few women he'd seen in the last few years were robust, Seraphina was a waif. She rubbed her arm absently as he approached her.

As she stepped back from him, she clipped him with a withering stare. "I think I have proven that I'm well enough. You need not stay here. I gave you my word I would help, that doesn't mean you are welcome to just remain here."

He came around behind her and removed the deep red cape that still hung around her neck. He hadn't removed it before laying her in bed the night before and she hadn't taken it off when she'd gotten up to get the salve.

"What are you doing with that?" Her voice, usually melodious, hit a crashing note and he froze. Did her waxy pallor mean she was cold all the time? The little cabin was like a Dutch oven, she should've been rosy with the warmth.

"I'm going to hang it up for you, then I'll check your provisions and make sure you're well taken care of. As I said, it's the least I can do after my horse knocked you to the ground."

"Provisions?" She took a step closer to the crate, then froze. "I haven't had much in the way of food purchased from the mercantile since my brother Martin left. He was the one to visit the store and I wasn't about to beg for Lenora's help." She crossed her arms over her narrow body, then flinched as pain shot up her injured arm. "I lived off the land. The Miwak live without flour and sugar, so can I."

Her bravado was beautiful, but a little flour and sugar wouldn't hurt her. She needed someone, anyone, to help her. She'd lived so sparsely, it could account for why she was so pale and wane. For now, that someone would be him since his horse had so rudely stuck him in her path. He approached her little crate with the curtain to conceal its contents and pulled it back to find her store of various leaves and one jar of dried meat that may have been rabbit by the color. He wondered how she caught it but wouldn't ask. Maybe her knowledge of the Miwak was deeper than he'd thought.

"This is all you have?" He gestured to her meager stores.

"Yes, it is sufficient for me," she answered in French, her voice clipped with anger. A pink hue suffused her cheeks, and he noticed tiny white marks on her skin, almost invisible. He averted his eyes. Though he had no idea how it had happened, he'd somehow hurt her by leaving the blankets open on the windows, though that was only a guess judging by how she'd quickly closed them when she woke, and the sudden appearance of those marks after.

He understood what she'd said, but struggled to speak French himself, apparently similar to how English was difficult for her to speak. He could answer her in English, and understand what she spoke in French. "It might be sufficient for you, but I plan to help you out for the next few days, so I'll need some provisions for me, too. As long as you're not opposed to gambling money, I'll go to the mercantile. Maybe I'll be lucky and see my sister there." He chuckled, but it held no humor. If he did see her, she just might get so angry it could hurt her or the baby as Seraphina had said. That wasn't any way to gain his sister's trust.

"I certainly hope you don't." Seraphina scowled and turned from him. "Her hurt and anger spilled over onto her husband and his feelings, now soured, will not turn. Trust me on this, he holds a grudge longer than most. You have a wide lake to swim before you see the reconciliation of your family. Victor alone will never allow you near her."

Her words punched him somewhere deeply. He'd known Victor would be angry. He'd been angry when he'd found Geoff right after his mother had died. "Are you worried that if I see my sister, my job here will be done and I'll just keep right on going? Are you worried I will leave you?" He hadn't felt like much of a man since he'd realized he'd abandoned his life. Taking care of Seraphina, even the little he'd done, rebuilt a part of what he'd thought was lost.

She narrowed her dark eyes at him and tilted her head, taking a full minute to answer. He wanted to be needed and would use his knowledge of cards and tell-tale signs to get her to let him stay, if he must. It was enough for her to want him to stay. Why bother remaining in Blessings if no one cared to have him there? Though his father had welcomed him, his sister was the one he truly needed to speak to, especially after his father had given him the little book.

"I'm worried about no such thing. If you leave, my life will go right back to being just the way it was, except I won't have to concern myself over stray horses or men showing up in my house, opening windows." Geoff felt the heat burn his ears. That hadn't happened in a long time. How often had he heard men speak plainly of the sporting women who were always nearby at a high-stakes game? He wasn't one to take what he heard to heart, yet he'd hurt her and that got to him. "I didn't mean to scare you or hurt you. I had nowhere else to bed down except the boarding house and I was worried about you." Not to mention the boarding house was a waste of money, and he had to make the little he had, last.

Her eyes sparked a momentary fear, then deep sadness he hadn't expected.

"Seraphina?" Geoff touched her wrist gently and she jumped as if she'd forgotten he was even there. That touched his pride. He wasn't normally one to be immediately forgotten.

She gasped, pulling away and rubbing the spot where their skin met, except it wasn't anger that flooded her soft features, but confusion. "I'm sorry. It's just, no one ever touches me. Not intentionally."

A life without any touch. The pain in her eyes and the power of her words nearly brought him to his knees. How did one live without any touch? Did it hurt her, or was she merely shocked he'd chosen to do it? He'd have to wait for his answer, because delving that deep into who the Frenchwoman was, would take far longer than he had.

"Will you be all right if I leave you for just a bit? Maybe you should lay back down?" He raised his hand to her shoulder and gently directed her toward her bed. "This is the time when you normally sleep, isn't it?"

She nodded absently and stood beside the bed, unwilling to even sit. "I won't be able to sleep if I lay here thinking about when you will return. Perhaps you should just go rent a space at the boarding house?" He felt the muscles of her shoulder tense as she asked, and again her brow furrowed with worry as she glanced at the door.

"Are you sure you would like me to do that? Wouldn't

it be nice to have someone around who can help you for the next few days until your wrist heals? Do what your brother did?"

She bit her lip and her eyes pleaded with him to stay, yet her mouth refused to agree. "Go."

He laughed, knowing he couldn't do that. He couldn't just leave her to deal with what his horse had done to her when she was so sensitive that a little light affected her. She'd mentioned too many times in passing that there was no one for her, for him to be just another person to leave her behind. "Trying to get rid of me so quickly? I may need to stay one more night, but I'll at least attempt to find somewhere else to stay." He smiled, donned his hat, and left. He'd expected her to want him around after being alone for so long and it was the perfect option so he could keep watch over her and avoid spending money.

Heat hit him in waves as Geoff left the cabin. People went about their business, ignoring him and everyone else as they toiled in their daily tasks. Men and women wore shades of brown, drab, blending in with the wooded surroundings as they worked. The closer he got to Blessings, the few women in the street wore colorful, perfectly tailored dresses while the men wore smart trousers, white shirts, and vests. At least he wasn't out of place.

Geoff wiped the sweat from his brow. He'd spent some months in San Francisco and the ocean had brought cooler temperatures. He'd forgotten how hot May in Blessings could get. The closer he came to the mercantile, the more attention he drew until he avoided the open stares of people as he strode up to its swinging doors.

Back in San Francisco, there had been men in the street, snake charmers in turbans and silk pants. When he'd come face-to-face with one, he'd realized he looked just like them. A foreigner, with his swarthy skin, dark brown hair and warm eyes like his mother's.

He pushed his way through the door to Ed's Mercantile and let his eyes adjust. A woman at the counter with dark, curly hair, pale skin, and fierce blue eyes fairly growled at him. "You." She shoved her money in poor Ed's face and lifted the hems of her skirt slightly to make a hasty exit.

"Don't leave on my account, dear sister." While they had never been close, her openly hostile bearing left him little choice but to be chilly in return.

"I'm sure I've finished all my business here, at least until Ed clears out the rabble." She pushed past him and let the door slam shut behind her. He wanted to chase after her, to explain, to make her see what he'd seen, but it was too soon for that. He'd done too much damage.

He took that moment to remove his hat, though the only two people left in the store were Ed Mosier and Atherton Winslet, the wizened owner of the whole town.

"Geoff Farnsworth? My stars," Atherton muttered. "Edward didn't mention you'd be returnin'." He scratched his chin through his long white beard. "Dare I say, welcome back?"

Atherton had never paid him any heed when he'd been there before, of course, he'd also been little more than a child when he'd left. "I'm not surprised he didn't mention it. I didn't tell him when I would arrive." He nodded to Atherton, hoping that was enough. He wanted to talk to Ed and get him to start putting together his list of provisions, so he could move on to the second task of the day, which was finding Cort and Victor. If it hadn't been hours since his horse had run, he could look. By now, the beast would be miles away.

Ed stood by the till, his hands resting lightly on the counter. He'd managed to put away Lenora's money while Geoff had been talking to Atherton and now gave Geoff his full attention.

"I need a few things, the usual provisions: flour, yeast, sugar, evaporated milk." And whatever else he could think of to put a little weight on her. "Maybe a sweet or two if you have any?"

Ed nodded and grabbed a piece of paper and swiped the pencil from behind his ear. He took down the list with efficiency. "And whom should I bill for this?" Ed's eyebrow rose in question.

He had to remember he was no one in this town. He'd given up any respectable name his father may have bestowed on him when he'd left, and his name certainly hadn't been respected where he'd come from. They didn't know him in Blessings, didn't trust him. "I've got cash. No need to start a tab."

Atherton came up next to him and gently rapped the counter with his knuckles, and looked like he was chewing on more than just what to say. "Jason didn't tell me we had any new guests at the boardin' house. Are you at the hotel?"

The old man hadn't changed. He was so observant he could practically tell how many hairs someone lost in the comb every morning, but that didn't mean he needed to know where Geoff had decided to stay. "I'm not at the boarding house, nor the hotel." He glanced around behind Ed and noticed two empty bright blue bottles. "Ed, are those for sale?" He pointed to them. All of Seraphina's bottles were just old, reused ones. She didn't have a single nice new one to put whatever it was she made in them.

"Yes." He beamed as he brought one over. It was a thin, rectangular shape, with some type of bumpy pattern in the dark blue glass. "Amazing how they do that." He set the bottle on the counter for Geoff to see.

"I'll take one of those, too."

The door swung open with a loud bang and all three men turned in unison as Victor stormed through the door. "Geoff Farnsworth, I gave you a chance to do the right thing. I told you to come back right after the accident, that your family needed you. You will not hurt Lenora further by staying. Get out, you lazy, good for nothing!"

Geoff held his hat in his hand, but didn't feel the need to cow to Victor, never had. "I've done a lot since then, getting wise in more than years. Last I heard, I don't need your blessing to stay here." He slid his glance to Atherton, but the old man just chuckled.

Victor strode up to him. When Geoff had left, they'd been roughly the same height, but Geoff now towered at least five inches over the Englishman. Victor hadn't been a fighter when he'd known him before, but he looked mad enough to throw punches now.

"You will not see her. Just the few minutes she saw you today was enough to send her to her bed. I will not have you—" He didn't finish. The dark fury in Victor's eyes threatened to erupt. He flexed his fists, his breath coming fast. Atherton crossed his arms, but didn't step forward to get involved and Geoff didn't want him to.

"At least I don't have to worry about whether or not you would defend my sister. I firmly believed you weren't good enough for her for a long time." Maybe he still wasn't if he held a grudge as Seraphina said, but at least he was willing to protect what he saw as his own.

Victor didn't say more, he nodded to Atherton and Ed, then strode out. Because of his coloring, Geoff had always dealt with people who didn't like him, but he'd never been shunned by family. However, there was someone he knew who had. Seraphina's brother had abandoned her, just as Geoff had abandoned his own and just as his family turned him away now.

Victor and Cort had been his only option in finding a place to stay that wasn't with Seraphina. He knew so few people in Blessings. If she truly didn't want him to stay, he would have to find lodging at the boarding house.

Atherton gripped his shoulder in a fierce hold. "Don't let it get to you, boy. Stick around and do what's right. They'll come around to your way of thinkin', see if they don't."

It meant he'd have to stay in Blessings longer, have a

cool head and not just run off and find the address in the black book. He would talk to his sister, if he just gave it time. And he would make it up to Seraphina. After he'd somehow hurt her skin by letting in some air, he owed her.

CHAPTER 4

T hough she'd spent her whole life avoiding the light, Seraphina couldn't get comfortable enough to sleep in the heat of the day, especially not after sleeping all night. It didn't help that she was jumping at every noise outside her cabin, wondering if Geoff would return. He'd claimed he would wait until the evening, but he had no reason to actually come back. Yet, she begrudgingly wanted him to. No matter what she told him, she was so lonely.

While the people of Blessings had never been overtly cruel to her—in fact, many had secretly come and asked for medicines or tinctures for various ailments—most avoided her, treated her as suspect, or even outright labeled her a witch. Just not to her face, and not with enough anger that Mr. Winslet would make her leave. She'd fought the battle too long to ever think she'd win. People feared what they didn't understand. No one was willing to understand her.

Her brother had told her while he was still there that those who avoided her, mostly miners and their wives, called her a witch. The people in town didn't think much of her at all. She never came to church, didn't go out in the daylight. When they did see her at night, she was pale and frightening. So, they avoided her. Martin had always said avoidance was better than being burned at the stake. At least they left her alone. She now wished she'd questioned her brother—asked him why he'd never defended her name. Maybe he'd liked that she was cloistered away. But if that was the case, why had he grown tired of her and left?

Geoff had closed the curtains, but just to be safe, Seraphina hung extra blankets over the windows. It would get warmer in the cabin all day, since she couldn't open the door or windows, but better that than to boil her skin with the sun. The discomfort of heat had always been preferable to the discomfort of the blisters.

She had just finished lighting her pot-bellied stove to make supper when someone knocked on her door. Instead of doing what she imagined every other person would do—go to answer it—she ran to the very back of the house. "Who's there?" she asked in her fumbling English.

"Geoff. Are you away from the door? Can I come in?"

He understood? She never expressly told him the sun had caused the marks on her, and even stranger, it didn't frighten him away. *"Oui, entrez vous,"* she mumbled. Geoff confused her. He was supposed to get what he needed, then move on. That's what all the other people of Blessings did. They got the help they needed, then avoided her, pretended she didn't exist. Yet he'd returned. Twice.

He pushed open the door just enough to allow himself and his paper-wrapped bundle in, then quickly shut it behind him. He smiled briefly at her, then doffed his hat and hung it on the wash stand by the door, just as her brother had done before he left. She'd lit one lamp to help her do her laundry in the dark room and the gentle glow made his bronze skin and brown hair warm and enticing, his curls tempting. Seraphina averted her eyes. There was no cause to have such notions about a man she didn't know.

"I hope you don't mind. I got enough to last a good long while. I happened to see Lenora at the store and I don't think this will be anywhere near an easy, or short visit."

She'd shared her tent for years with her brother, and even the cabin for a very brief time before he'd left. So she didn't mind letting Geoff stay a few nights, but she did not want to share her cabin with a stranger indefinitely. "And you think because you've purchased a few things that you can just come in here and sleep where you will?"

He'd disrupted every minute of her life. It didn't matter that she'd desperately prayed for that very life to change—this wasn't what she'd asked for.

"I can't afford to stay in the boarding house. Not without going back to my gambling ways or begging from my father and I'd really like to avoid both, at least until I convince Lenora to talk to me. She would use gambling or taking advantage of Father as excuses to ignore me. He doesn't have room for me there, or I would stay with him." He set his bundle down on her table and pulled the twine knot loose.

Lenora might not ever talk to him anyway. Talking to Geoff would open the wound of losing her mother. Seraphina had helped many people in Blessings heal from many things—from blisters to wasp stings, burns to ax gouges—but she couldn't heal anguish. She didn't even want to try. She had enough of her own to try to heal.

He clenched his hands and leaned against the table. "Though Atherton didn't say anything that would lead me to believe I'm not welcome in Blessings, I sure feel like I was being told without words to leave. The stares." He shook his head. "These people live right next to a quiet Indian nation, yet they see skin slightly darker, and stare." He stood tall and scraped his hand down his handsome face. The shadow of a beard had sprung up along his jaw overnight, outlining it with noble lines.

"They probably don't even realize they do it." She'd told herself that very same lie for years. People stared at her, too, when they managed to see her at all. She'd gotten pretty good at avoiding them as much as possible. Because she was allowed to stay, she'd always assumed there wasn't any malice behind the stares, or that it was minimal.

"I know you'd rather I not stay, but I've got nowhere else to go. Your brother's bed is still there in the corner, it just needs to be set back up. I'll cut wood, gather meat if you've got a gun, make meals, do your shopping.

Whatever your brother used to do, I'll do it. Just, please don't ask me to leave."

She didn't have a gun, so if he needed one, he'd have to get it from somewhere else. All the other things would be welcome. She'd missed her brother, not so much for his companionship, because he'd been no companion, but because of the help he'd offered, not to mention the protection. She needn't worry about anyone showing up at her door during the day, because no one came while he was at the mine and he had taken care of it when he wasn't. There was very little reason for them to even see each other all that much, as she would usually sleep during the day while he would be awake.

"For now, you may stay," she told him. "But you'll have to find a way to get your own weapon. I have never owned one."

He set to unwrapping the package. "I didn't see any at the store. Maybe you have to ask to see them, or he doesn't have any right now. A place as out of the way as Blessings doesn't always carry every item a person needs all the time. Now, if I was back in San Francisco, then I could go to almost any store and get just what I need. Of course, I'd also pay five times for it what I would anywhere else." The smile slid off his face. "You can buy just about anything in San Francisco, whether you should or not."

What did he hope to gain by talking to her? She glanced over at him from across the small room. Though he gave no outward appearance of nerves, he continued to talk of inconsequential things. She replied to calm him.

"I only remember the noise. We came ashore at night and it was barbarous." She shuddered. "The worst of humanity, come out to play." She could still hear the noises of the brothels as they'd driven through town, and various other sounds that had sent shivers up her spine. Noises she'd refused to think about or revisit.

"Everywhere you go you can find evil. Humanity is humanity." He didn't look up from his task and didn't hear her gasp. Was that why he tolerated her company—because evil was everywhere? Did it cease to bother him, because of its prevalence? In that case, maybe he did think she was just as evil as the town did.

"And do *you* find evil in Blessings as easily as you can in bigger cities?" She moved away from the hot stove, unsure whether her light head came from the heat or worry over his words. Yet, the weight of hope pressed down on her that he didn't assume such things.

"As I said, people stare here, just like they do anywhere else. I've got no right to say if a man's heart is good or evil. I can only read the face he shows me."

She tentatively crossed the few feet to where he stood by her table and glanced over the fare he'd purchased. "Thank you. It's been a long time." She touched the small sack of flour but couldn't meet his eyes.

"Are you worried, Seraphina? Do you think the people of Blessings see you the same way you saw people in San Francisco?" He stilled, and she stared at his hands where he leaned against her table. They were so large compared to her own.

"How could they not? They don't know me. Just like I

can only assume actions by the noises I heard as we drove through town in the dark, the people of Blessings only know of me what they've heard."

"Then perhaps it's time they knew more?" He dipped his head and tried to catch her eye, but she turned away. Her cabin was safe. What if she did try to come out and they were terrified? What if they did try to make her float with weights on her ankles or any of the other horrible things she'd heard people did to witches?

"I can't. When I go out, people are terrified. They look at me and fear for their lives. I'm surprised they even use my medicines, that they aren't afraid I might poison them."

Without warning he touched her arm. A warmth like she'd never known spread up from the spot. No one deliberately touched her, yet he kept doing it. Voluntarily. She turned her head and his warm brown eyes finally met hers and held them captive.

"Their ideas of you will never change if you don't teach them otherwise. Miners tend to be superstitious. In some ways, it keeps them alive. You can't just live out your days in this cabin with no one to talk to and no way to get meat or—"

She yanked away from him and his notion that she was helpless. "You have no idea how long I've lived on my own. More than two years. I've survived on my wits and the help of the Miwok. No one in all of Blessings even knows I've spoken to them. I trade herbs from this side of the river for things they have on their side. Many are happy to trade."

He laughed and the crinkles by his eyes made her belly flutter. "You see? You prove me right. If you talk to people, reach out to them, they have no reason to see you as different."

Hadn't he just come from town and threatened to leave because of what people thought? Did he not see his own duplicity? "What excuse do you have? You came back here telling me you want to leave because of how the town stared at you. What makes you so different from me?"

His laughing eyes darkened and she stiffened in the wake. Though he was still handsome, unease made her take a step back.

"Unlike you, who can change what people think of you just by talking to them. I cannot. My skin is what makes people distrust me, and despite efforts by a certain privateer in the bay," he spat and sneered as his voice lowered to a menacing rumble, "I can't be stripped of that."

Though she had no idea what he meant by that, he was an ally, something she hadn't had in a very long time. The world had dealt him false just like her. She couldn't let that go. If it meant she had to deal with having a strange man in her house for a brief time, so be it. In a cabin so small, he wouldn't be much of a stranger for long.

CHAPTER 5

eoff pulled the last of the contents from the small paper bundle of provisions he'd purchased, hiding the little bottle behind the sack of flour so Seraphina wouldn't see it just yet. His mood had shifted from optimism at finding an supporter, to cloudier than a Coastal California spring. While he may have been pithy in his comment to Seraphina about his skin, just the mention of that day made him itch. No one would ever see him so much as roll up his sleeves again.

Ten months before, a slave trader, a dealer in flesh, had Shanghaied him while he'd been drunk in a dark alley behind his favorite saloon. He'd been taken aboard ship, but they hadn't left port, when the captain decided he would do what he could to keep Geoff aboard. Geoff had been furious, and insisted the captain let him go.

He'd tried to escape and the captain had set to making an example of him by proving that *scum* like

Geoff didn't bleed the same. He'd been stripped and flogged on the deck as the crew laughed. They'd thought he couldn't move as he lay on the deck, raw from head to toe. They'd let him be for just long enough and he'd jumped the gunwale into the bay.

The shock of the water had almost killed him. With all the boats packed in so close, he'd been able to quickly swim between two moored nearby. When he was sure they wouldn't find him, he hid. If a kind woman hadn't noticed him almost immediately from her spot on the deck of her house boat, he'd have bled to death in the murky water. He still wasn't sure how he hadn't. She hid him and tended his grisly wounds, and she would be the last living soul to see them.

Her kindness—and fondness for a family who would never take her back—had finally softened his heart to his own kindred, where all the years and the death of his mother had not. Miss Rosa, his rescuer, was a former prostitute. She'd made her money in a brothel during the big boom of '49. Her family would never forgive her, nor see her as anything less than a tarnished woman, especially since she'd chosen the profession after her husband died. There weren't many professions for a woman that earned a better wage and she'd been desperate to pay debts. Her empty boat was the perfect place for her to hide from the world and come and go as she pleased, so she'd made it her home. Which had been lucky for him, since, if anyone else had found him they may have just left him to die.

When he was well enough to walk again, she'd gone

off her boat to a store for some new clothes and a hat for him. He'd lost his gun and everything else when the captain had stripped him, but at least he was alive. Miss Rosa had given him twenty dollars, kissed his cheek for good luck, and sent him on his way.

That twenty dollars had multiplied as he'd played poker, starting small and moving to high-stakes, until he'd won over a thousand dollars and a horse. The very horse that led him right to Seraphina. Unfortunately, the thousand dollars didn't seem like much when it might have to pay his way by rail all the way across the country to a family that might welcome him even less than his Blessings kin.

His conscience nagged that a woman shouldn't be forced to think on such things as changing someone's skin, no matter how futile. "I'm sorry. Forgive me for planting such images. I had no right." He dipped his head. Though he felt no shame over what happened, only anger and contempt, it was wrong to force her to see him as he was—forever scarred and ugly, because he'd run off and lived by his own wits. Only three places on his body remained untouched by the lash, his face, hands, and feet. Everywhere else stayed covered at all times.

"You say you cannot change your skin, which is true, but changing what someone believes about you is just as difficult. I am able to trade with the Miwok only because I offer what they would have to otherwise break their treaty to get."

He prayed she didn't endanger herself, or the rest of Blessings, with her coming and going. "Doesn't the treaty work both ways? They are not to come here, but we aren't to go there, either." He could remember enough from his short time in Blessings that the only enforced law at the time was the treaty. No one dared break it. No one wanted to start a war and there was no reason to provoke a peaceful people.

She turned up her narrow nose and sniffed delicately. "I don't hurt anyone. I give them the plants they want, they give me the food I need...what I don't catch myself."

"Yourself?" Curiosity got the better of him. How was a woman who had no weapon to catch anything?

She knelt down, concealing herself with the volume of her black skirts. He caught the slightest glimpse of her delicate calf in black stockings before it was again covered by her skirts and petticoats. His heart raced as he averted his eyes to what she held. She lifted a rough dagger, spun it deftly, and handed it to him, blade pointed to her own heart.

"For a woman who just met me, you're certainly trusting." He took the blade by the hilt. The craftsmanship was good, though old, and she'd kept it sharpened just as he would. "Where did you get it?"

She took it back from him and set it on the table. "It's all I have left of my family. It was my father's. I was told that the stone set in it means something, but since I'm all that's left, I'll never know if it's true or not."

The woman—who he was more and more certain by the minute was no witch—certainly had her share of secrets. "So, you use that blade to catch your supper? That's quite resourceful." He couldn't help the slight mocking bent to his voice. While a knife might help her if some drunk miner found her out wandering in the woods, how would she ever manage to use it to catch food?

She narrowed her eyes at him and in the blink of an eye picked up the knife, flipped it, and flung it at her wall of tinctures. With a solid *thump* it sliced into the wood and held there, vibrating for a moment, exactly between two of the bottles. They didn't even wobble. She turned back to him and stared with unblinking eyes. "I didn't get the rabbit from the Miwok."

WITH GEOFF's eyes slightly bulged in surprise, Seraphina wanted to laugh, but held it at bay. If she allowed him to know her, to see her for the soft-spoken, easily hurt woman she was, he might take advantage. Though he seemed to be nothing like Lenora had described him, Lenora was Geoff's sister and would know him better than anyone. As much as her need for companionship made her want to trust him, to see the goodness in him, she couldn't ignore what her only friend had said.

"You caught a rabbit with that knife?" He finally spoke, slowly, with his jaw a little too loose.

"When you're alone, you make do with what you have." She strode over to the blade and yanked it from the wall. "It isn't the only thing I use. I've used rocks—"

"Wait, you've killed game with a rock?" He turned to

face her, his hand at his waist, forehead lined in confusion.

"No, against Cort Nelson."

Unexpected color filled his face. "What did he do?"

Even her own brother had never concerned himself much with what people in Blessings said about her, yet Geoff stood stiff, looking like he was ready to run out and pummel the livery owner. "I thought he was beating a child in the woods after dark. The child turned out to be a woman, and he wasn't beating her. He," She averted her eyes from his intense gaze. "He married her."

"In the woods?" Anger melted to shock and disgust on his face. Geoff was just as expressive as his sister.

"No, as I said, I hit him with a rock and almost killed him that night. He married her about a month later. At least, I think he did. I wasn't invited to the ceremony and she hasn't come to see me since. When she decides she wants a baby and needs to improve her fertility, then she'll remember I'm here." She reminded herself that she couldn't have gone to the ceremony anyway. It had been during the day, when she couldn't really go out. Though, she had braved the daylight for Cort's Hannah when she'd needed her medical help. Hannah had been hurt in the jail by a man everyone had assumed was a lawman. The doctor had been out of town. Hannah's absence since then hurt more than others, because she knew Seraphina would never hurt her and, unlike Victor, Cort didn't dislike her.

Geoff leisurely approached her, it was only a few steps, but seemed as if he crossed an ocean for as slow as his movements were. "You know Cort by name, you know Victor, and my sister. How many people of Blessings do you know, who don't know you?" His eyes sought hers and the room, though already small, closed in on her. Other than Lenora, none knew her secret, and none would care. They never could know. If they did, it would be impossible to convince them she wasn't a witch. Though, from what she'd learned, people knew very little about the opposite side of Christianity. They often attributed anything they couldn't understand to darkness, sorcery, witchcraft.

"I know the Joneses, Mr. Farnsworth, Ed from the mercantile, The Abernathys, the Nelsons, the Edwards, and many others. People don't hesitate to come and get remedies from me. I don't know how they first knew about them, but maybe that's why they think I'm a witch." That and the fact that she rarely went out in the daytime.

"All these people know you, know you're willing to help them, yet they don't bother to even ask you who you are and why you keep such strange habits? I've only been here a day and I would do that for you."

Yet she prayed he didn't. He was now the only person who spoke to her and though having him staying with her wasn't how she'd planned to slake her need for companionship, if he now left, she would be alone yet again. "Lenora knows. Even when Victor forbade her from coming to see me, she did anyway, though she hasn't in quite some time. Not since she told me of her coming family."

"If Lenora was your closest friend—"

She had to interrupt him again, no matter that it was rude. "She *is* my only friend."

He sighed and started over. "If Lenora is your only friend, you must have heard some terrible things about me before I got here. What do you think now?"

Geoff had been a gentleman from the moment she'd made herself known in the woods. He hadn't been selfish as Lenora claimed. Lenora had said he never thought of anyone but himself. But from what Seraphina had seen, he'd either changed or had never been that way to begin with.

"I think you are less selfish than Lenora claimed you were."

He laughed. "In fairness to my dear sister, the last she knew of me, I was. Utterly selfish. I took her dreams and threw them in the refuse heap because I didn't want them. I left because it suited me and I didn't come back, even when I should've. But in my defense, if I had stayed, become the good son my father wanted, I would still be drinking every night to drown out the screams in my head. I can't stomach the idea of becoming a lawyer, of sitting in an office all day." He shook his head and turned from her as his shoulders fell.

"Maybe I'm still selfish."

Desiring a bigger dream was what coming to California was all about. It didn't make him selfish, just an opportunist like everyone else. "If you were, you would've left the witch on the ground and chased your horse."

He took a deep breath and let it out. "I've got a long

way to go, Seraphina. I don't always do what's right, not by a long shot. I want to do the right thing, but only if it means that I don't have to stay and become my father. It isn't that he's a horrible man, I just..." He threw up his hands then went back to the table where he'd left his small stack of provisions. "I may not be thoroughly selfish, I did get you this." He held up a small blue bottle with a cork top. She'd never seen anything quite so beautiful.

"Why?" she asked as she reached for it. With her little lamp, it looked both black and blue in the soft light.

He handed it to her, his warm fingers grazing her cool ones. "I guess I was just thinking about you while I was shopping."

He wasn't a horrible man for not wanting to be his father. He was a man all on his own. "You don't have to explain your reason for leaving. I understand. Lenora told me she'd wanted to be a lawyer, but her father wanted you instead. Now, she doesn't want to because it would mean leaving her husband to go to school. Neither of you want to do it and Mr. Farnsworth doesn't seem any worse off for it."

He glanced over at her, but she could not meet his gaze. "I'd bet giving up her dream didn't make her hate me any less."

If anything, it had made her angrier. "She needs you to set her straight. You are a convenient excuse. Until she releases that anger, it will continue to grow."

He crossed his arms, but said no more. No man was completely selfless, but this one had done more growing than she'd ever thought possible after hearing his sister's account. She just had to get her friend to see it.

In the distance, a loud bell clanged and Geoff glanced all around. "What's that?"

"It's the fire bell. Something in Blessings is burning."

He ran for the door and slapped his hat on his head. "They may need my help. Don't wait up for me." He dashed out the door but remembered not to fling it wide.

He may not have gained all the wisdom of some men of the same age, but he was trying and if he helped the town put out a fire, then they would soon see the change in him. That meant he would move on from her more quickly. She gripped the back of her kitchen chair and said a prayer for his safety, and that he would come back to her.

CHAPTER 6

The clanging of the fire bell didn't stop as Geoff ran down the hill, collecting other men as he went. He didn't need to go ask anyone where he should go, it was obvious. Smoke poured from behind the livery, even from as far away as he was, he could see it. Men gathered in front, some releasing the horses into the front corral, others forming a bucket brigade. If they had to go from the livery to the river, the whole place would burn. There wouldn't be enough men without the miners.

All those years his mother's voice had been like that smoke, prodding him where to go. Like the smoke, it had been without substance, but real to him nonetheless. He'd spent five years running from that smoke, running from what was right. Running from work and responsibility. Now, he could see the right path, because she'd prodded.

Thank you, Maman.

A man with a glinting badge stood near the corner of the building where the smoke emanated, pointing men to where he wanted them. As Geoff made it to the front of the line the man looked him over for a moment. He had a large scar near his ear and hard, dark eyes.

"Geoff Farnsworth, where do you need me?" he said, answering the unasked question.

"Sheriff Pete Jones, Go on and get in the bucket line. Fire's not bad yet, but the pump isn't fast."

Without waiting for more, Geoff ran off down the line. The more men they could find to join, the faster the bucket line would be. Cort waited at the end of the line, pumping buckets of water from a central well.

"Geoff, here, pass these on." He handed a bucket and kept right on working.

Since there weren't enough men yet, he had to run back and forth until the line filled in, finally leaving him next to Cort and passing the buckets without having to move. A boy ran from the building back to Cort, returning the buckets.

"Do you see if the smoke has stopped?" Cort didn't look up from his pumping job to check for himself.

Geoff leaned forward to see around the long line. His back strained against the movement. The livery was situated on a flat plain, just outside of the town, and seeing down the line wasn't easy with all of the people in the way. Pete Jones and Victor made their way toward Cort.

If he didn't ask Cort about a room just then, he might not get the opportunity. Victor would never allow it.

"Cort, I know you've just been dealt a turn, but I'm in town and willing to work if you've got a place to bed down. I could help you rebuild whatever part of the livery burned."

Cort flexed his hands and grimaced. "I've got nowhere to put you up. The section that was on fire was where the sleeping loft was. I'd be glad of your help with the repairs, but is there anywhere else you can stay until it's completed?"

Seraphina didn't want him there, but he'd have to plead with her once again. Staying at the boarding house and the hotel would put him very close to the saloon and he'd rather stay away from those places if possible. Not to mention his growing concern for Seraphina. She was far too much like him to simply walk away.

"I think I can find somewhere." Geoff shifted to stretch his aching muscles and watched as Atherton broke ranks with the bucket line and followed Pete and Victor the rest of the way to Cort.

The sheriff spoke up first as the men created a loose circle. "We got the fire under control. What happened?"

Cort leaned on one hip and took a deep breath. "I found a young boy I didn't recognize behind the livery, smoking a cigar. Since we keep some hay back there, I told him to go on. He got scared and dropped the cigar into the hay. I thought I'd doused it with enough water, but it must have smoldered all night and in the heat of the day, finally lit."

Atherton clicked his tongue and shook his head. "How much damage?"

Pete shrugged and nodded to Victor. Victor frowned and crossed his arms. "I'd guess it will take us a good couple days to fix it. In the meantime, we'll have to keep the horses on the undamaged side of the barn or out in the paddock."

Cort glanced around the group. "Geoff has offered to help us with the repairs. I've already accepted."

Victor gave him a hard look, but didn't fight Cort over it. "If he wants to pick up a hammer and do some real work, so be it. But he stays by the livery, nowhere near my house."

Geoff stepped forward to defend himself. "I did not ask to come to your home, only to help if it's needed. Do you deny my help?" Working with Cort and Victor would give him another reason to stay, beyond Seraphina.

"No, I don't deny it. I was simply stating that it won't change my opinion of you."

Atherton cleared his throat. "You found somewhere to stay yet, Geoff?"

He truly hadn't yet and the hospitality of the Winslets was legendary, but he didn't want to stay there. He couldn't keep an eye on Seraphina if he was with Atherton and Millie Winslet. They might not even approve of where he'd been staying and he'd didn't want to bring more attention to Seraphina than necessary.

"Yes, staying with a friend, sir." He wiped his aching hands down his trousers and flinched. He didn't have any spare clothes and he needed a wash.

"You come and see us if you need. Edward has been my friend for too long for me to leave one of his kin out."

Atherton turned to leave the little group and headed back toward town.

Victor took a step back from the group. "We'll be starting the repair work tomorrow, best be there early, Geoff. If you can manage to get out of bed before the sun hits its zenith." He walked off and Geoff let the slight to his character go. Victor would eventually be turned, but not with angry retorts.

"You up for this?" Cort laughed. "I hope you know what you're getting into. It's going to be at least two days of back-breaking labor and putting up with Victor in his snit."

Geoff laughed, but it wasn't humorous. Cort was right, the next few days would test his metal. "I can manage to ignore Victor. It won't be the first time."

"Nor the last." Cort laughed and headed back toward the livery. All the men of the bucket line had dispersed, leaving Geoff to head back to Seraphina's, even though she didn't want him. He'd told her he might not be back, but there wasn't anywhere else for him to go and they'd managed to get the fire under control faster than he'd expected.

He first headed to the river to wash the sweat off his hands, face, and neck. He might not be able to wash his clothes, but at least he would be able to wash the worst parts. In the next day, he'd have to think of a way to get more clothes, but for now, he'd have to settle with going back to Seraphina's and convincing her to set up her brother's bed once more. He would need it for at least two days. After that, was anyone's guess.

CHAPTER 7

After Seraphina washed the bedding and set up her brother's old bed for Geoff, she sent him outside to hang it. She'd lived her life alone for years and, while having him in her cabin wasn't an intrusion, it did make the cabin feel twice as small, especially now that it was certain he had to stay for a few days. He wasn't a great burly fellow, but he was tall, almost hitting his head on the rough beams that held the peak of her roof. He got the job of hanging the blankets completed far too quickly and soon came back inside.

He'd come back from the fire at just past the noon hour and she was still wide awake from sleeping when she usually didn't. There was far too much left of the day and she couldn't lay down to sleep when Geoff sat at her table. He held her dagger in his hand and wiped the whittled scroll work on the hilt with his handkerchief. She set to finding something for them to eat, since her thoughts scuttled around the room too quickly to do anything that required sitting.

"Seraphina, come look at this." Geoff glanced over at her and offered a slight smile.

She didn't want to—she would rather avoid him. He hadn't done anything to incur her anger or avoidance, he simply made her feel something akin to confusion. She couldn't put a name to what she felt when he looked at her. Slowly, she abandoned her search for something to cook and stopped at the edge of the table.

Though she'd owned the blade for many years, she'd never really taken the time to look at it. It was a tool. Her father had taught her to use it and her brother had insisted she keep up practice. Though, that very act had allowed her brother to walk away. Her spine stiffened at the thought. He had done just what Geoff had done. Did that mean there was hope Martin would return someday, and did she want him to?

"Yes?" She refused to look into those honey eyes, instead focusing on the hilt he'd so lovingly polished. The wood, which had looked almost black to her, was now a rich brown and the carving could be seen easily. She'd always cared for, cleaned and fussed over the blade, but the hilt with its links to her past, she'd kept distant.

"The leaves and flowers are a work of art, but what's interesting is the family crest, right at the top." He pointed to an oval point just below the blade. "If your family was given this dagger, it was by someone of great importance. If it was passed through your family, then you may be part of a bigger family than you think."

Seraphina dug deep into her memories. *Maman* and *Père* had lived alone. Though many of her friends had large families, hers was small. "If I do, they are lost to me. I don't remember anyone but my parents and Martin, *mon frère*."

He tugged her down into the chair next to him, his eyes wide and earnest. "Aren't you at all curious? What if someone in France holds the key to who you are? Doesn't that fascinate you in the slightest?"

All the years since she'd left with Martin, she'd prayed that they would end up somewhere with plants or a doctor with the expertise to help her, but family might hold the secret. Nowhere they'd landed had such people. Dr. Edwards, who cared for the people of Blessings, had taken a tentative look at her when he'd first come to town since Martin had asked him to, but he had no answers, and didn't return. She'd made herself sick over and over testing out the local plants for something that would stop the sun from burning her, but every test had failed. Anytime she got so much as close to its heat, she burned.

"What good would it do? If they exist at all, I would have to go back to France and search high and low. If I had family, they didn't care about us. We were alone, poor, and hungry, though we always shared what we had. If there was any wealth in our family, they didn't see fit to share it with us." If there had been wealth, *Père* may not have died, and if he hadn't, *Maman* certainly wouldn't have.

"I'm sorry, Seraphina. I've come to think of family as this object of ultimate importance. If I somehow find a way to bring us back together, I feel like something of great value will be gained."

He had every right to be excited and hopeful, but she couldn't afford to be. Martin had been gone for years and she hadn't received so much as a letter telling her he'd made it wherever he'd decided to go. Geoff's family lived just down the hill, whereas hers were across an ocean—if they existed at all. Many of the local French *gendarme* would assume her father had stolen the dagger from someone important if she ever sought wherever the crest came from. They would simply take her into custody if she asked about it. Being a family who helped those who slept on the street made them a target of scorn. Only derelicts of justice would help others in the same situation.

Seraphina gently took the blade from Geoff's fingers and turned away so she could put it back on her thigh, where it belonged, secured from anyone else. She could forget about it when it was there. Dreaming about far away family didn't make the sun move in the sky any faster, nor did it make her nerves calm.

Geoff joined her near the little stove and stood behind her as she searched through the food he'd provided. He eyed the various vegetation she had hanging in the corner.

"That doesn't look like anything I've seen in the store."

"I doubt you have. It's a root that has a sharp taste, but when broiled on top of meat is quite good."

"We'll have to deal with the lack of meat in this house tomorrow. It's a little too close to supper for me to go and find something now. I'll start with Ed's and see if he carries at least a pistol. If he doesn't, I'll go ask my father. I doubt he hunts, but he must eat somehow. I remember he had a rifle before I left."

Seraphina nodded, though she didn't much care how other people got their food. She hadn't had help in so long, she'd take Geoff's, no matter how uncomfortable he made her feel. "So be it."

He reached around her and she held her breath to keep as still as possible.

"I think some parsnip soup will have to do." He tugged a few of the long carrot-like vegetables from the wall. "I'll go wash these if you want to start some base on to boil."

Her brother hadn't known the first thing about cooking. She turned and watched Geoff's eyes dance with his teasing. He knew he'd surprised her. He gave her a quick, brilliant smile that left her far more breathless than it should've, donned his hat, and left her to deal with her nervousness all on her own.

GEOFF KNELT BY THE RIVER. Though it was a good long way from Seraphina's cabin, he needed the break. Being around her did strange things to his sensibilities. He scrubbed the turnips and tried to focus on the task, but he kept picturing dark golden eyes and skin too light to be healthy. Did being in the sun make her skin change, or was she sickly? Did he need to call in a doctor for her?

His horse had hit her hard and he'd never met her when he'd lived in Blessings before to know if she was usually that pale. Or had the damage to her wrist left her looking that way? He just couldn't be sure. His sister would know, though.

Leaves crunched behind him and he sat up on his heels to glance behind. Victor stood a few feet away, his arms crossed.

"Geoff," was the only greeting he offered.

Geoff was thankful he hadn't rolled up his sleeves to do the task, even though it would've kept his shirt dry. Victor didn't need to see his ugly scars and question him about them. He nodded and went back to washing.

"Where are you staying?" Victor barked from his spot. "You wouldn't tell Atherton, but I need to know you're not staying at the saloon."

"I don't see that it matters." Geoff tuned his ears to the sound of footfalls. If Victor meant to shove him in, he'd be ready.

"Lenora wants to know. Despite her anger with you, she heard from Edward that you're not staying there. Now she's worried. I don't want my wife worrying."

Geoff took a long breath. There was still hope, to fulfill his mother's wish that he come home and build back his family. If his sister was concerned, he might be able to break through to her. "My horse knocked Seraphina Beaumont down as I was coming into Blessings. I'm staying with her until I can be certain she isn't hurt. Lenora can find me there if she wants to see me."

"You're staying with the witch?" Victor spat, his cultured English accent lacing every word. Victor only let his roots show when he was riled. Why the mention of Seraphina angered him so much was a mystery, but one Geoff couldn't broach until he'd seen Lenora. He hadn't expected Victor to have such venom for a woman Lenora considered a friend, unless Seraphina was mistaken and thought there was a friendship there that wasn't.

"Yes, and according to Seraphina, she and my sister were fast friends."

"I forbid her from going there now. I will not have my child hurt by that woman."

The turnips kept him from balling his hands into fists as he wanted to. "You never did see people for who they were, only for what they could do for you. You haven't changed much in five years, Victor. Somehow, I expected the influence of my sister to make you a better man. It seems I was wrong."

Victor came forward a few steps and Geoff stood to his full height, to remind Victor that he wasn't just a boy anymore. He was now taller than his father, lean, and very capable of defending himself—or Seraphina.

"You talk to me of becoming a better man? What of you? Where have you been? Off dallying with women and cards? Five years, Geoff. Five years you stayed away when your family needed you. Five years Lenora had to deal with the loss of her mother on her own. Five years she had to look out for Edward. Where were you?"

Guilt dragged down his shoulders, but he wouldn't let Victor know. "I don't need to be disciplined by a man who ran out on his own family. Who left England to find himself, and never returned. At least I came back."

Victor stared, his jaw hard, but Geoff had him. Victor could call himself a good man now because he was married, owned half of the livery, and was about to become a father, but he'd done everything Geoff had, only bigger.

Geoff relaxed his arms. "I'm not trying to shame you, Victor, I'm not your enemy. But you aren't any better than me. I'm here to rebuild my family. Blessings is the key. But if Lenora won't see me, then I've got the name of my mother's family from Father and I'll try to rebuild what was lost there. Family means too much not to." The stripes on his back, earned because of that very family, were proof of the importance of his blood. It had earned him hatred, but could it earn him love, too?

"My family forgave me," Victor mumbled. "I didn't have to go back home because they forgave me. I'll do what I can to get Lenora to see you, but don't count on it. Don't even expect it, especially if you stay with that woman. I won't let Lenora visit there."

He cast his eyes at his feet and his bluster left. "It wasn't your fault that your mother jumped, but Lenora," The words seemed to stick in his throat and he didn't finish.

Geoff knew. He'd known since Victor had accused him of running away the first time. Since he didn't come back to Blessings, he'd brought on the anger and hurt that Lenora couldn't place anywhere else.

"I accept that I hurt her. I'd like the chance to tell her

66

I'm sorry. I want to start over. I'm sorry for other things I did as well. Some men never get the chance to say those things." Some men got Shanghaied and never got free. He'd been one of the lucky ones, even though it was hard to see it that way. "I've had to go through a lot to get to the point in my life where I can say that, but that's why I'm here. I don't mean to cause Lenora strife."

"I'll let her know where you're staying and maybe she'll want to see you just to find out how Seraphina is doing. She can visit you while you work at the livery the next few days if she chooses to."

Good, at least Seraphina would have one friend once he left, because Lenora would never stay away from a friend completely. Yet, that didn't offer the comfort he hoped. Victor touched his hat and strode off. Geoff stared at the clean turnips, wishing he knew what to say to Seraphina about Victor's appearance. It would only hurt her to know Victor was keeping her one friend from her, and hurting Seraphina was the last thing he wanted to do.

CHAPTER 8

Geoff took long strides to return to Seraphina's cabin. Though his time with Victor provided a small victory, he wasn't even close to winning the battle. He touched the handle on Seraphina's door and stopped cold. In his excitement to share his news, he'd almost flung her door wide. He had to learn to control himself better or he'd have to stay forever. His actions without thinking would continue to hurt her. He certainly couldn't leave until he'd made it up to her for not only knocking her down but for leaving her curtains open. Why that was a bad thing was still a mystery, but perhaps one of her medicines made her skin burn if she was in the light. She hadn't told him, and he hadn't wanted to press her for answers.

As he opened the door, he stuck his head in to make certain she was far away, then continued. She was over by the stove at the far end of the little cabin. There was a pot on the stove and steam already poured from it.

"I was beginning to wonder if you'd decided to move on." She tapped her spoon on the edge of the pan and indicated the board on the table where he should put the turnips.

"I took a little extra time because Victor joined me beside the river for a bit. We had a talk about Lenora, and you."

She turned to face him, her eyes wary. "Whatever could you have had to say about me?"

There were so many things, but none that he knew for sure, not yet. "I told him I was here with you."

She interrupted him, "And do you think that was wise? You know how they feel about me. Lenora hasn't come here in months. The town only tolerates me when they have a need. If you wanted to mend the pasture as you say in English, then you've started all wrong."

He laughed, not because it was funny, but because it took him a minute to understand what she meant. "I think you mean 'mend fences', and yes, I know what I'm doing. I'm staying with my sister's good friend who needs my help. Unless you'd like me to leave?"

He hoped she didn't. Though people would wonder, the quarters weren't any closer with Seraphina than he'd been with other women in the last five years. The cot where he'd healed at the hands of Miss Rosa had been in the same room and closer to her own bed than Seraphina would be. The sleeping quarters on her boat were much smaller than Seraphina's cabin.

She didn't look him in the eye as she took a knife from the small box by the stove and strode around him. If she wanted him to go, he would leave. But she wouldn't answer.

"Well?" He watched her pick up a turnip and deftly peel it.

"You have nowhere else to go, correct?" She still didn't look at him, but it was probably better that way. The knife she used to peel the small turnip was huge and he held his breath, praying she wouldn't lose an appendage to the glinting tool. He could stay with his father and sleep on the floor if he must, but that also meant he'd have to tell his father that he would not stay, would not become a lawyer. His father might still see him as a failure then, and he'd be unwelcome. It was best for that to wait until he was ready to leave Blessings altogether. For that reason, he'd been avoiding a second visit to see his father.

"No, not really. I suppose I could work for someone at the boarding house to earn my stay, if I have to. But I've already agreed to help at the livery," he offered. He didn't want her to feel as if she must keep his sorry hide around.

"The livery? With Victor? He'll never let you stay there. Then I see no other way. You will stay here until you must leave." She lined up two of the peeled turnips and sliced them so quickly he hardly saw the knife move. Other than providing her some food, he would be no help in the kitchen. Her skill with a knife would leave a lesser man uneasy, but worse, her choice of words didn't sit well.

"I asked if you'd *like* me to leave. I didn't ask if you

felt obligated." He waited to see if the gleaming knife would hold still for just a moment so she would look up at him.

She froze. "Ob-li-gate-ed?"

He'd have to teach her more English if he stayed with her. "Yes, when you feel you must do something, because of duty or honor."

"You think I have honor?" her voice was barely a whisper and she stared down at the food, though her knife remained still.

"Of course I do." He sat down next to her now that her knife had stopped. "You help the people of Blessings, even though they've given you nothing in return."

"They don't ask me to leave. It's more than other towns." She lifted the knife to start and he held up his hand to stop her.

"But it proves that you're willing to do the right thing."

She nodded slightly. "You may stay, not out of *obligated*, but because you have offered to help me and I need it." She went back to chopping and he decided not to correct her.

He would help her, not only with getting meat, and in learning more English, but perhaps he could eventually get the town to see in Seraphina what he did.

She stood and gathered all of the turnip rounds into her apron, then went to the stove and put them into the stock she'd started, probably with some of the dried rabbit she had available.

"You know, I could help you learn more English. Maybe you could even help me remember some of the French my mother taught me."

Seraphina lifted the lid on a tiny pot of salt and took out a pinch, then put it in the soup. "Lenora was teaching me before, but it was only so that we might talk easier. Now that she doesn't come, I see little reason to learn." Her words left an ache in his heart. The thing the reoccurring dream of his mother had impressed upon him was a loneliness that only someone who knew him deeply could quench. Family. Seraphina hadn't had that for so long. She had the same need he'd had.

"What about me? If I'm staying around for a while, don't you want to talk to me?" He laughed, hoping she would relax. She'd been quite tense since he'd returned from the fire.

"I am getting along fine with you, no?"

"Yes, but you live in California. Don't you want to be able to someday walk confidently down the street and talk to anyone you'd like? You could live anywhere you want."

She'd been stirring the soup, but stopped. "I'm sure the men from the saloon would love to stop and talk with me. They are the only ones I would see. Worthy people don't wander around town after the sun goes down."

"Obviously some do. And nothing is stopping you from changing your habits. Go out during the day and meet people, they are not all that frightening." He had to know if it was the absence of sun that kept her so pale or if she really needed the help of a doctor, perhaps even because of her medicines. She wasn't trained, so it was possible she had taken something that hurt her. He refused to let her think she wasn't respectable because she had chosen to live her life at night.

"Geoff, I know what you are saying, but you don't understand. The people of Blessings know who I am. They know enough about me that they shouldn't think less of me, but that doesn't stop the talk. Nor is it any less of a fact that I *must* live at night, when all the decent people are asleep."

But why must she? What wasn't she telling him? He'd hoped he could shift her schedule a little bit, because he wasn't ready to stay up through the night to keep her company, especially since he had to be up with the sun to work. He was already tired after his night on the floor.

"You've gone out before with your cape on. You said you'd helped people and your cloak would protect you."

"Yes, I've gone out before at my own risk. I chose to in order to help Hannah, Cort's wife. But would you attempt something you know will hurt you? Perhaps I am too cautious, but I don't know how people would react if I was to simply walk outside."

Her own risk? Did she really fear that people would hurt her for coming to town? Hiding away in her cabin wouldn't help the town see her as anything more than what they already thought.

"What about the evening? People are still out. Would

you risk going out then?" If it was merely the people she feared, then the evening would still be frightening.

"I do go out in the evening, but I wear the cape and gloves. I need light to be able to collect the plants I use in my medicines. Usually, I can manage to stay out of the way while I do my tasks."

The cape and gloves would hide who she was from anyone looking at her. He glanced up at all the medicines and tinctures along the wall. All gathered so others could benefit. But what of her? There had to be more to her fear, some reason she was so certain people would hate her.

"After supper, I will rest for a while, then resume my nighttime schedule."

He had no call to stop her. Her life had gone on just fine without him in it and he couldn't ask her to change just so she could be trapped in her cabin all day. A darkened cabin that already felt like a prison after he'd only been there one whole day. How could he ask her to move around her schedule so she couldn't even go outside like she did in the night?

After a quiet meal, Seraphina did just as she'd said, she laid down in her bed and soon her breathing evened out to a sleeping rhythm. When evening came, he would open the curtains to let some air move around in the little cabin. It was stifling in there with everything closed and the stove cooling now that it wasn't needed.

He glanced around the little cabin and forced himself to avoid letting his eyes wander to Seraphina's side. Next to a rocking chair sat a crate and atop the crate was a book. He sat down in the rocker and picked it up. It read *La Bible* on the blue leather front. Seraphina had a few verses marked and notes all along the edges in beautiful handwriting, though he could only pick out a few words, one word kept popping up across the pages. It was the same in both French and English—secret.

CHAPTER 9

It had been more than a full day and Seraphina wanted to check her shoulder and wrist. She glanced over to the corner where Geoff slept soundly. He'd been awake for many hours and she'd had to wake him from where he slept in her rocker to go to his bed. Since then, she'd waited to do anything until she was certain he was deep in sleep.

That time had arrived.

She slowly peeled the top of her dress down and checked her shoulder. It was a dark bruise, but didn't appear serious. Her wrist, while still painful, could move normally. After fixing her dress, she went to her wall of tinctures and found the bottle she was looking for. Almost empty.

There were some plants that grew in a small corner of the forest on the far side of Blessings that would help heal the bruising on her shoulder and perhaps even soothe her wrist, but she hadn't collected them in some time. She would need more than she had, but her small stock would give her time to make the tincture.

She slipped out the door and closed it softly behind her. The evening, when the only sunlight to be seen was filtered through the trees, was perhaps the most dangerous time for her to be out. Yet it was necessary. If she picked the wrong plants, by choosing to only go at night, she could poison herself. By sticking to the far outskirts of Blessings, she usually avoided people. She wove farther out into the trees, avoiding the noise of the town until she found herself about eighty yards behind the homes of Atherton Winslet and his sheriff, Pete Jones. She glanced over to make certain neither sat out on their back stoop. When she was sure she was alone, she pressed on.

After a few minutes, she heard a whistle. It came through the trees, the jaunty tune sounding like it could have been military or made up on the spot. Seraphina ducked within a copse of trees, waiting for whomever headed her way to pass. If she didn't hurry, she would miss what little light was left.

The man stopped right by her hiding spot and the whistling slowed, then he stopped and he laughed. "You can come out. I saw you pop in there from way back. I don't think we've had the pleasure of ever actually meetin'." She recognized the craggy voice of Atherton Winslet. She'd always wondered if the reason she wasn't swiftly run out of town was his doing.

Seraphina slid from the shadows of the trees and

pulled her hood down lower over her head, hiding in it as much as possible. "No, we haven't."

"Well, now that's a shame. You lived here almost since the beginnin' and I knew Martin well. He was a good worker. Just disappeared on me one day. I hope nothin' happened. I don't remember who was mine security at the time, but they should've come to check on him. I've come to your door to give you his final pay, but there's never an answer."

If he came during the midday, it was likely she hadn't heard. She'd learned to sleep deeply all through the day.

"When I saw you walkin' back along the edge of the property, I got his pay out of my desk and decided to give it to you. Thought you might be needin' it." He held it out to her, but thankfully, didn't come closer.

She reached out and took the heavy envelope, then slid it into a pocket inside her cape. "Thank you. I didn't know he'd left behind anything. I hope he didn't cause a bother." Like he had caused her. When he'd left, it had upended her life. A woman unable to go out in the light held very few options.

"Minin' is hard work and we lose people right often. Some collect their pay, some might not even realize they have it comin'. I couldn't just forget it, knowin' you were still there in that cabin. You gettin' on all right?"

She wasn't sure how to answer him and she glanced quickly at the tree line before hiding deeply in her hood once more. "May we walk as we talk? I have very little time."

He chuckled and motioned for her to continue, then

fell into step next to her. "I am doing well. Geoff Farnsworth has been helping me the last few days." She flexed her fingers under her long gloves, the bulge from her wrapped wrist making it difficult to bend.

"Oh, is that right? I wasn't sure where he was stayin'." Atherton scratched his beard and smiled as he glanced skyward. "That boy was a powder keg when he left, but he seems to have run out of steam now."

Atherton's words were confusing, and she tried to understand what he meant. English had so many meanings for different words and understanding Atherton, with his strange way of speaking, was difficult. "He's here to see family. I just got in the way of his horse as it ran off on him."

"I wondered who that horse belonged to. It's been at the livery for two days and Cort just don't know what to do with it."

"I'll let Geoff know." They reached the small clearing where her plants grew and she took a deep breath. The air was loaded with the various leafy fragrances and the tang of plant death as the old fed the new.

"I'll leave you to your gatherin'. I'm glad to finally have that money delivered. Take care, now." Atherton touched his hat and made his way back the way he'd come.

It was easier to hide from the direct light on the ground and Seraphina lowered herself until she knelt, then searched for just the right plants. When it was almost too dark to continue collecting, a crashing noise came from behind her. She stood quickly and searched for a place to hide, but she'd crawled to the center of the clearing and the nearest tree was quite a few yards away. If anyone found her alone, would they hurt her? She'd only helped others when she'd been certain they were in too much of their own need to ever bother with her. But she was nowhere near her cabin to run and hide if the person proved less than friendly.

Geoff stumbled into the clearing, panting and holding his side. "There you are! I've been searching everywhere. I was worried you'd listened to me and gone into town. I couldn't ask anyone, in case you hadn't, but I didn't even know where to begin. I came upon Atherton and the strange old coot didn't even wait for me to ask, he just said you were up this way."

He panted, now that he'd gotten his story out, as he made his way to her, then sat down in the grass. Seraphina sat down, unable to think of what to say. Her own brother had never worried where she was or what she was doing. He'd never concerned himself with how the townspeople saw her. Why would Geoff? What did she owe him that he would worry over her?

She reached into her cape and drew out the envelope, handing it to Geoff. "I don't know what the provisions cost, but you can take it from this." She didn't know the words in English and switched to French.

He laughed and glanced inside the envelope. "Where did you get this?"

Would he think she conjured it? She feared doing anything, lest people think anything evil of her.

"Atherton gave it to me. It was my brother's. He has been trying for three years to give it to me."

Geoff handed her back the envelope without taking any money from it. "Well, you shouldn't have had to wait that long and I think I've figured out the answer. Not only to the problem of the town, but so I don't have to worry about you. I'm going to teach you how to write in English, so you can write notes to people when you need. We'll hang a box outside your door and I'll hire a boy to check it every day and deliver the notes."

A system to communicate with others. A bridge. "What about after you leave? Someone may be willing to come to my door while you stay there, but not when it's just me. There's too much fear." It was worth considering, though. Geoff had proven himself trustworthy. Perhaps even with her most painful of secrets. But only if she could be sure he wouldn't change his mind about her. She had to be certain he didn't think of her as a witch before she could do that.

"It's a start. First, we need to teach you some words. My *maman* taught me French by making me memorize lists with meanings, we'll start with things in your home."

Lenora had started similarly, but she'd only taught her the spoken word, not how to write them.

"Then you can teach me the same lists in French. We can learn together." He smiled at her, his breathing finally back to normal.

"I'm sorry you ran all over Blessings for me." The sun dipped behind the Earth and she finally took a deep releasing breath. The sunset was her freedom from the shackles of her skin. All day, she had to suffer in the heat of her stifling cabin, and at night, she could not see. The few minutes in the evening, she could take off the layers that concealed her and live normally.

She shrugged off her hood. In the graying light of sunset, Geoff's eyes widened and he reached for the flower behind her ear. She'd forgotten it was even there until he plucked it from her pin.

"There. You don't need the bright flower, you are enough of a flower yourself. When you show your face... you glow." He smiled sheepishly, then glanced away.

His words touched the broken places in her heart. He thought she was pretty? She'd worn the flower to give her color, beauty. It was so much a part of who she was, the very fragrance of who she was, she felt naked without it. Only in winter did she go without, and most of winter she spent indoors.

"Did you find what you needed out here?" He handed her back the flower.

She stared at it, the pretty petals garish against her black gloves. "Yes, I found the plants to help my shoulder and wrist, but I do need to get back and brew them."

His head tilted. "Brew them? Like a tea...or?" His voice faltered.

"I don't own a caldron." She stood quickly, grabbing her basket of plants and headed back toward home. Why did he have to assume she was what she'd insisted she wasn't? Him, the one who had appeared to understand her the most.

"I didn't mean it like that. Seraphina, wait." His

footfalls rushed behind her and he gently grasped her elbow to stop her. "I don't see the worst in you. Can you see better of me?"

"If you weren't going to accuse me, why did you stumble over your words?" She yanked her elbow from him.

He sighed and his eyes softened. "Because I don't know the right words in French. All the more reason for us to teach each other."

She hadn't really considered his offer. No one in Blessings would write her a note. With the exception of a grocery list, she had no reason to write to anyone. But if she could talk more easily with Geoff, maybe it was worth it. He led her back toward her cabin, but didn't say more, what he'd already said gave her enough to think about.

CHAPTER 10

After Seraphina had walked with him back to her cabin the evening before, he'd stayed up with her the entire night. They'd worked out a word list by pointing to various things in the cabin. She wrote down the name in French, and he wrote in English so they could both learn from the same sheet. After staying up so long, he wished he could crawl into his bed instead of washing his face and going to see his father. But the visit couldn't wait, he'd need clothes by the end of the day.

Seraphina had yet to admit it, but she needed him. Without him, she couldn't shop for food, wouldn't even get to know the town. She was stuck in her tiny cabin and stuck in darkness. Yet, when he'd seen her in the sunset the evening before, she'd taken the breath right from his lungs. It had stopped up like a cork. In the shadowy light of her lamp, she'd appeared so thin. He wanted to see her healed of her fear of people, then healed of whatever made her so pale, so he could show the town just how beautiful she was.

He glanced at her form lying on the bed across the room and took a deep breath. He couldn't see anything except a small lump, hidden under a light sheet. The day would be warm and the inside of the cabin stifling by midday with all the windows covered in thick blankets, yet she still covered with a sheet as if she couldn't bear even the slightest hint of light. Or perhaps she hid from him? He averted his eyes, because he had no claim over her despite what his heart kept telling him.

She'd said she wasn't a witch, but her habits were difficult to reckon. It made sense that she wore her cape to hide from the notice of people, but if that were all of it, she wouldn't be so secretive. If only she would explain to him why she did so many of the strange things she did. Trust might be forthcoming once he worked to gain it by teaching her, if he could manage to stay up so many hours and work.

He didn't have a tie, but he made sure his collar was buttoned properly and brushed the dust off his trousers. Geoff would ask his father if he still had the clothes he'd abandoned when he'd run off. They may not fit well, but he might be able to pay to have them altered. It would be better than having only one set. Every man needed at least something he could put on for wash day.

He left the small cabin, allowing Seraphina to sleep in peace without him, and made his way down the hill toward town. Many people were up with the sun and though it was barely light, were outside on their way to work or going about their business. Geoff hadn't really noticed people doing things like that, normal things, in a long time. Where he'd lived, men slept away the morning after spending too much time at the tables the night before. If he'd never left Blessings, he wouldn't have been caught in that alley and he wouldn't have to pull on the wrists of his shirts to make sure he was covered at all times. As much as he questioned Seraphina for staying hidden, he had the same issue. They both hid from the prying, inquisitive eyes of others.

His father stood outside the Land and Law Office with a broom, sweeping the walk. He'd never witnessed his father perform any sort of manual labor. He'd always been a man of few hours of sleep, and Geoff was glad he'd continued the habit. *Maman* had also been up with the sun, but not once they'd come to Blessings. The memory pushed him forward to rekindle what had been lost.

"Good morning," he called as soon as he was certain his father would hear without having to shout. His father turned from his task and waved, then set the broom against the wall.

"Good morning to you. I wasn't sure when I'd see you again. You showed up in the dark of night, then disappeared. If I didn't have Victor and Atherton telling me they'd seen you, I would've thought I'd dreamt the whole thing." He tugged on his vest to make it lay flat. His father had lost quite a bit of weight since Geoff had left and he was now tall and thin. His eyes had once been blue and bright, but were now gray like the ocean on a dreary day.

"I came to talk to you now, briefly, before I'm off to help Victor with his repairs." He hoped his father would see the offer as growth, not as running away from him yet again, but the visit had to remain short. He had to have a way to provide for Seraphina while he stayed with her and the livery was that way. He refused to even consider taking her money, no matter that she'd offered it. She would need it once he was able to move somewhere else. Hopefully by then, she would have met a few people and feel comfortable with them to ask for help getting her a list from the store, or she might even go herself.

Edward pulled open the door to his office and held it for Geoff. He hadn't been on the main floor of the Land and Law office in over five years and it had changed much since he'd been there. Lenora's desk used to sit right by the front window. It had been neat as a pin, despite the fact that it was little more than boards set atop some crates. Now the space held a bookshelf. Father's desk sat just where it always had, at the base of the stairs. There were two ways up to the house on the second floor, the indoor stairs from within the office, and the outer ones up the side of the building. When he'd left, there hadn't even been a store next to their home. Now, the outdoor staircase was hemmed in by the Land and Law Office and the clinic.

"I'm surprised to see you here so early. The Geoff I knew could barely be roused by ten."

Back then, he'd had no respect for the life he'd been

given, didn't even realize how well he had it. "I took advantage of the fact that you were my father and I would never have a need. I let my feelings control me. I've done a lot to change." Hopefully enough for his father to overlook his past, yet still understand he had his own life to lead.

"So you say, but you still haven't said why you're here. I assumed if you wanted to just talk, you'd have come for supper yesterday." His father crossed his arms as he leaned against his desk.

Geoff stared at the strange sight of his father's completely clear desk. Though he'd always been neat, there had been stacks of paperwork to do, files to put away. An empty desk meant nothing to do. He'd never thought it possible, but was his father out of work?

"I came to see if you still had any of my clothes, but now I'm concerned for you. Lenora's desk is gone and yours is neat as a new penny."

The older man's eyes closed and he sighed. "I didn't want to burden you with it. I know you have no interest in taking over. I'm getting old enough that I don't want to keep working. Atherton has asked that I keep the office open until another lawyer comes to Blessings, but I'm ready to be done. I'm ready to sit on my porch and watch people live their lives."

If he hadn't left, Geoff would've gone off to school and come back, then trained with his father and he could've quit working. His father could've had the peace he desired at the expense of his son's, but perhaps that was what sons were supposed to do. "I'm sorry, Father. I never wanted this job, but I don't like seeing you worry, either."

"I don't do much anymore. The land has been doled out for years, all I do now is take care of sales when one family sells their plot to another. Now that there's a full-time preacher at the church, I don't even do the weddings anymore. Blessings has grown, and I've been glad to be here to watch it, but I'm not needed here anymore."

Blessings might not need him, but certain people in Blessings did. "Now you're ready to sit back and watch your grandchild," Geoff filled in. "What will you do if a lawyer never comes?"

Father shook his head. "I'm not sure. My desk is clear for now. Atherton will have the final say, he's older than I am and still working. I'm sure if anything happens to me, you could fill in. I hope you recall what I taught you."

He did, but he'd rather nothing happened to his father. Working *with* his father would've allowed him to see the man he'd grown to miss, and that was the only draw. It might even entice his sister into seeing him. Taking over without his father would be detestable.

Edward took a deep breath and closed his eyes and smiled slightly. "Thank you. I'd hoped with your desire for family that you would stay. Lenora will come around, so you won't have to go seek your mother's family. She wouldn't let you. It's just her way. She's angry right now and stewing about it, but if she thinks you'll leave, she'll come running."

"I don't want her running. I just want to see her, other than yelling at me to leave." The mercantile didn't count.

He'd surprised her and she hadn't known his intent, might not have even known he was in town yet. Maybe it wouldn't matter, but he'd hoped once she learned why he was there, she might be more open to forgiveness, and starting over.

"Give her time."

He couldn't leave, not until he'd completed the work he'd promised Cort, and not until Seraphina was healed. Then, despite his father's hopes, if he was still unwelcome, he'd have to move on. "Father, did you keep my clothes from before?"

His father nodded. "You didn't stay here long, and I'm not sure they will fit you, but everything that was yours is still in your trunk, upstairs. You're welcome to it."

Geoff nodded and headed up to his old room. After so many years, he wasn't sure where to even start with his father, but at least the question of following in his father's footsteps was now answered. He couldn't. The room he'd lived in for such a brief time was at the top of the stairs and down a short hall. He opened the door and covered his nose and mouth against the thick dust. His sleeping palate had been removed and all that was left was his trunk. His father had closed the door and left it be. Probably since Geoff had left, as he'd had the loss of Mother to deal with.

Within the chest he'd brought with him to Blessings, Geoff found three sets of clothes with enough fabric to be adjusted and an old pistol he'd forgotten about. It needed to be cleaned, but it should work for his purposes. Geoff stuffed all the items into a sack and went back downstairs.

"Atherton mentioned you'd lost a horse. They've got one over at the livery that they found a few days ago. No owner has shown up for it yet," his father told him.

He'd heard similar from Seraphina and had planned to ask them. He would need that horse if or when he decided to move on, but he hated the idea of keeping it at Seraphina's, especially with the way it had treated her. She still had to wrap her wrist and he'd noticed her rubbing her shoulder when she thought he wasn't looking. He'd managed to hurt her and he owed it to her to stay and help. He'd hurt a lot of people. The realization that he needed to mend fences with his father stopped him in his tracks. By leaving, he'd told his father that the life he'd chosen for his son wasn't worthy.

"I'm on my way there now. Thank you, and I *am* sorry, despite how it may seem." The words were surprisingly easy to say once he'd decided to say them, and he did mean them.

His father shrugged slightly. "I can't fault you. I would be handing you a business with almost no work. You wouldn't even be able to support yourself. What kind of father would I be if I wished that on my son? A poor one. Go, but be sure to come see me for supper one night." He waved as Geoff left the building.

How long had his father known the business couldn't be passed down? Yet he'd stayed away for that reason. He'd sacrificed time when he could've stayed. The hot sun poured down on him just as the hot truth had. He'd ruined the last five years for no reason, caused a chasm that he couldn't see across with his sister, and missed his own mother's funeral and burial, because he'd been selfish. With so much to make up for, how had he ever thought his time in Blessings would be quick?

CHAPTER 11

The day was almost fully spent when Seraphina woke. She'd tossed and turned after Geoff left, wondering what he would do with his day. Since he hadn't told her, dreaming was about all she could do.

She had no reason to believe he would stay after he'd spoken to Lenora. Once that connection was re-forged, he could leave and write letters to his sister and father. Not her. Even the few days she'd known him, he hadn't seemed to fit in the spirit of Blessings. Some wanderers came to stay, like Cort and Hannah Nelson, others moved on. Geoff seemed like the type who would need to wander.

The list of words lay on the small table next to her rocker where her Bible usually sat. He had to have been studying it before he left, as she'd put it next to his seat at the kitchen table. Even after such a short time, it had become his seat—not Martin's. Her brother wasn't going to return. Sitting down in her rocker, she took up the list and glanced over it.

She'd struggled so much with telling Lenora her secret, had fumbled over her words. Telling Geoff would be even more difficult. She'd known deep down that Lenora was a friend, someone who may or may not take her explanation, and friends could come and go. Though Geoff had said he would leave, the thought of having him leave because of her words tore her apart. If he judged her falsely because of her ailment, and her inability to explain it clearly, it would haunt her for life. If only there were a way to practice her words, or even to present them clearly the first time, she mused, tapping her cheek. With enough time and practice, she could write a note to tell Geoff her secret. She could then get the words just right, but how would he take them?

Even Lenora—who had never thought she was a witch—was skeptical about her ailment. Lenora made sure not to let light in if she came to visit in the evening, and when she'd asked Seraphina to come help her during the day, she'd understood her need to cover up. But there was still a hesitancy there, a disbelief. *Everyone* burned under the sun's light. It would be difficult to convey the severity of the burns without putting herself through it to prove just how bad it was. In so doing, she would probably seal her fate as a known witch. So the only way was in a note.

Geoff had offered her options to visit the town, had pushed her to try, but he didn't understand. Knowledge of who she was, truly, scared people away. Even people who were supposed to love and care for her, like Martin, couldn't be trusted to care. What would it be like if Geoff believed her? If he knew her secret and didn't run, if he defended her as no one ever had? What then? Everyone deserved a champion in their life, someone who believed in them, no matter the foe. It wasn't as if she'd expected her brother to climb in a lion's den, like Daniel. She'd only asked him to care. Perhaps that was too much to ask of anyone.

Three quick raps on the door, and Seraphina was up and out of her chair. She rushed to the back of the cabin in case it was as early as she suspected it was. Geoff peered in and smiled.

"Good. I'm glad you're up. I've been working all day, now I need someone friendly to talk to."

She hadn't even prepared coffee for him and she scrambled to get a pot on. He looked exhausted after his night awake with her, then toiling all through the day. "What kept you all day? Is the damage so bad they keep you until night?" If he'd met with his sister, instead of working all day, his remaining time with her could be short.

"I visited my father early this morning. I have a feeling he'll close up soon. I don't know if he'll stay in Blessings, but I would guess so. Especially since Lenora is here."

She'd never considered that Edward might leave. He was a part of Blessings. "I thought parents tried to stay close to their sons. What if you move on, isn't it likely he would follow you?" She had to know his plan, yet, he'd been hesitant to tell her anything. She slowly poured the ground beans into the pot, more intent on his answer than what she was doing. She could almost make coffee in her sleep.

"I don't think so. I offended him pretty heartily when I left. I feel like he's glad to see me, to know I'm alive, but he wouldn't follow me."

A pang for her own parents touched her heart. If only she had the option to see them and talk. "I'm glad. Perhaps you'll find that you want to stay near him? And Lenora?"

Geoff removed his hat and laid a bag on the floor near the door. "Perhaps. I don't know what I would do in Blessings permanently, though I would have the same issue no matter where I land." He lifted the list of words and scanned it. "Have you been awake for a while? I didn't expect you to be."

The heat in her cheeks could easily have come from the steam of the brewing coffee, but it was also possible it was from his words. He'd been the one to get her up, even though he hadn't even been there at the time. "I had trouble staying asleep." She stifled a yawn at the thought. A few more hours would've been nice. The coffee would do her good.

He went to her small storage box and pulled out the two mugs. "Well, I'm glad. When I told you I was staying with you, it was to watch over you while you heal, not watch over you while you sleep."

If only she could simply tell him. If she only knew all the right words and could do it in a way that wouldn't confuse him. Yet her brother's betrayal hurt deeper than she'd ever thought, and he'd known of her ailment all along. Had he left because he was tired of people and what they said about her behind closed doors? Martin Beaumont could be anywhere, but it only mattered that he *wasn't* there, with her, where he'd promised to stay and watch over her.

"Seraphina?" Geoff touched her arm and again the warmth shocked her. "Are you all right?" He turned her from the stove to look at him. "I've been standing over there, talking to the walls apparently, because you haven't heard a word." He chuckled, his eyes cloaked in concern.

"I was," she bit her lip, considering her words, "thinking. Nothing to worry about." Again her face flamed hot.

"There is certainly nothing wrong with thinking. Care to tell me what was on your mind that kept you from hearing me?" He moved the pot off the heat and drew her over to the table, careful of her wrist.

She sat in her chair, and when he was seated she took a deep breath. If she told him her secret, or even showed him, then he wouldn't need to wonder about her strange behavior anymore. He would know that she could only go outside fully covered unless it was the deepest evening or night.

"I..." No. He was too new to her. It had taken months for her to take Lenora into confidence and even she hadn't taken the matter seriously. There was no way Geoff would understand after such a short time. Not when she'd been shunned and labeled falsely in other places before Blessings. Her little cabin on the side of the mountain had to remain hers, or she would again be cast out. "I was considering what I need to do to make the tinctures with the plants I collected last night."

He cocked his head, as if he'd just discovered something funny, or knew she'd lied to him. "How do you get the alcohol to make them?"

His curiosity confused her slightly, but at least he was interested. The bottles were easy to find. The whiskey she usually used wasn't. She'd had to convince Ellie at the saloon to sell her a few bottles. Her brother had always done that before. So many things she'd taken for granted. She should've thanked him back then, but had never considered it. He'd just done what needed to be done.

"I purchased a few bottles from Ellie. She is willing as long as I have the money."

"And has she ever treated you strangely?"

Considering she'd had to wait until Ellie came out to add to the trash heap, and she'd caught the saloon owner unawares, yes. "She wasn't prepared to see anyone waiting outside for her."

He nodded and his dark eyebrows rose. "So, it's possible you didn't bother her at all, just caught her by surprise."

"It is possible, as you say." Yet it didn't matter, whether Ellie, Lenora, Hannah, or any other women from Blessings were willing to overlook her strange behavior, it still wouldn't change that she couldn't befriend people who lived during a separate set of hours than she did. It didn't change what her brother had said—*"The people of Blessings, like everyone else we've encountered, think you're a witch..."* And so she stayed hidden.

He stood and poured two cups of coffee then brought them back to the table.

"I'm not trying to make you uncomfortable, Seraphina, only to make you think. You wanted to know what kept me out until it grew dark? I was working at the livery. It will be a good place temporarily, but I can't see myself working there long."

It was another reason to leave and she just couldn't bear that yet. "I'm sure if you're meant to stay, you'll find what you're searching for." Seraphina clutched the cup in front of her and prayed he could speak to Lenora and that she would want him to stay, prayed that he would come up with meaningful work that would keep him in Blessings. With her. She'd already started thinking of him —wondering about his past and his future, though none of that would matter if he packed up and left.

"I'll find something. I can't just stay here and live off your generosity. I've lived off of others for too long. Perhaps finding a solid job, something respectable, would help both my father and sister to see that I'm not the wastrel they think I am. Something beyond the livery and mucking out stalls after hammering nails all day."

"Wastrel?" That was a word in English she hadn't heard. Most of the time, she could easily figure out what Geoff meant, even if there were words she didn't understand.

"I was a gambler, a drinker. I avoided my family and their problems. I should've taken those problems on myself, lightened their load. If I'd been a man, I would've."

She understood, he was using a word to describe himself much like Lenora had. "That life brought you back here," she pointed out. He had come back to make things right and that was something she couldn't overlook, not with her past. Just because he'd made a bad choice once, didn't mean his whole life was a poor choice.

"Only by force. Until I'd almost lost everything, I didn't see what I'd thrown away." He glanced at his pocket watch. "Take a walk with me for a few minutes before I have to go to bed?"

The question left her staring. Lenora had always wanted to stay inside once she was there and hid as she left so no one knew it was her when she came and went. "You...aren't afraid to be seen with me? What about doing things that are respectable? You just said you wanted your family to know you were serious."

He nodded and grabbed her cape from the peg and offered it to her. She held up her hand to stop him. "I will go with you. But for once, I'll leave that behind."

It was already dark enough that she needn't worry about burning, but perhaps she could take the first step away from her fear of everyone in Blessings—if Geoff was by her side. If he was willing to be seen with her, and risk the town's reaction, then maybe she could face the same.

CHAPTER 12

Geoff led Seraphina down by the river to walk. Her red cape, though meant to conceal her, had actually made her more visible in the night than her black dress. Without it on, he could hardly make out her form in the darkness and shadow of the trees. But for her pale face, he would have doubted her presence, even with her standing right next to him. The moon cast little light to catch her features.

He wouldn't have called her beautiful when they had first met, but now he saw her beauty. It was bound in her frailty, her softness, her concern for others. When her brow furrowed, he couldn't stop his own from mirroring it. He'd cared for women in the past, certainly for Miss Rosa who pulled him from death's door, but he couldn't understand the soft caress of desire he felt for this woman. Not a burning desire to have her, but one to keep her, encourage her, feed the growth in her very soul until she became the knowledgeable, kind woman hiding beneath the veil of her cloak. He wanted the world to see the woman who had once been cloistered from everyone's view.

Didn't he owe it to her to do that?

But what of himself? If he did that for her, wouldn't he find himself completely trapped by her grace? He'd already begun making decisions based on her needs. If he continued, the tenderness he felt now could swell to something that would engulf him. Though he knew little about love, this he could sense. She bent and plucked a white flower, then tucked it behind her ear. Almost instantly, her face seemed to glow more brightly, as if the moon suddenly knew just where to reflect.

He'd asked her to walk, but now realized he had nothing to keep up the chatter that kept him from sounding as inept as he felt. He was a man of the world, who had walked away from family and faith to live a life of high-stakes. She was a woman who didn't leave the forest around Blessings. She may have come all the way from France, but her life was tethered to the town. Could he agree to stay, if it meant he could help her forever? His wanderlust had been strong five years before, but now?

She glanced over at him and he caught the brief gleam of her smile in the moonlight. It was so rare, he wished he'd caught it in the lamplight. He chuckled, because he could think of nothing else to do. She was a mystery to him, one he wanted to solve, yet the call to family was so strong.

Seraphina may never want to add to her own family, perhaps she only wanted to replace the brother she'd lost. Even if she *did* accept him, let him be there for her, she may never fully let him in on the secret she kept hidden in her Bible. That would keep him from ever fully knowing her. Her secrets would keep them apart, and keep her from ever questioning why he couldn't be more to her. He couldn't love her as a husband, even if she would eventually trust him, because then he would have to show her his scars, something he'd vowed to never do.

He'd helped her in so many ways. If he continued to offer her assistance and friendship only, she would never see his scars. She would never have to understand him fully, because that burden was heavy and he couldn't saddle her with more. He could love her, but from a distance.

In order to stay, he'd have to convince her he wanted to. They'd spoken earlier of permanent work and that would keep him in Blessings. "I think I have an idea." There was one profession he could have that would allow him to travel, yet he would always return. "Perhaps Blessings needs a boot and leather store." He would have to go buy hides or gather them himself, but Geoff was confident he could learn the trade. Part of him still worried about the future, and Lenora. If he started a business, he would be bound to Blessings. He couldn't have the family he desired with Seraphina and if Lenora never let him in, he would be giving up everything just to stay.

Seraphina turned to him for a moment then continued walking. "If you started a shop, you would need to stay here."

At first he would, and he might not be able to start it for a while, but once it was going he wouldn't be tied to Blessings, but he would be tied to the land nearby. He would never be able to go as far East as he would need to go to find his mother's family. Still, he could visit all over California, hunting down places that would sell him quality leather. His father had taught him how to run a business. He could hire someone to work in the shop while he traveled.

"I would, but only for a time. I could talk to Atherton and my father about investing in the equipment, but I think that would be minimal and I do have some savings that I'd kept aside in case I needed to keep traveling." He scratched his chin and kept walking. The longer he stayed out with Seraphina, the easier it was to talk to her. "The more I think about it, it's perfect. It's a respectable job and there's a vacant building on the corner of Main Street." Maybe he could find some happiness in just having something to call his own, a business he'd created.

"But is it a skill you know?" Seraphina stopped in a pool of moonlight and it caught her pale skin, illuminating her like an angel.

"I don't, yet. But a man who wants to learn isn't far from his goal." He wanted Seraphina to believe in him, to tell him he could do it, that he should stay.

"I can help you, but you'll need leather from cattle, tough leather, not from deer. It's too soft."

He nodded, glad of something they could talk about at length. "And do you know about tanning and preserving?" Though he wanted to keep her right where she was, she continued walking.

"I do. My brother would hunt deer for hides and meat and he bought cowhide from nearby ranchers. I added decoration, then he would sell them. Men paid good money for it."

Men in San Francisco had worn boots with intricate stitching on them, not work boots, but fancy colorful footwear. He'd always wondered how it was done. "Do you know how to dye it?"

She cocked her head and considered his question. "I don't, but I'm willing to learn." A smile lit her face. "I've never had a job before. Would you hire me?"

His heart tripped. He'd wanted to stay to see her release her fear of others, offering her a job would be a start.

If she were to work for him, he would need her to be there while he was, so he could oversee her work. He couldn't be up all day and night as he had been. "I would need you during the day, though."

She stopped and turned away, back the way they had come. "I'm afraid I can't. I want to help you, but you'll have to find someone else." She wrung her hands as she stood waiting for him to decide if he would follow her or go off on his own. Would it really matter when she worked, if he got her to do it? He was already exhausted from trying to stay awake as many hours as he could to be with her, and she also looked tired from doing the same.

"Seraphina. Would you please tell me what is the matter? I've been there when you're awake during the day, so I know you're able. Please, just tell me what your reason is for avoiding the daylight. Surely you see that it's the only reason people have for thinking you're strange. They have nothing else to go by."

She twisted her fingers even harder until he wanted to stop her. Was it so difficult to tell him the truth? Was he so untrustworthy? His sister didn't want him around, and Seraphina couldn't trust him. She'd looked like an angel in the moonlight, but his mother had told him that even the demons knew Jesus was Lord. Was he fooled by a pretty face? Did she say nothing because what everyone said was true? He didn't want to believe it.

"I cannot go outside in the daylight," she mumbled.

But just the evening before, he'd watched her remove her cloak in the evening as they'd sat in the grass. It may not have been full day, but she had been out and it was light enough to see her beautiful face.

"I don't understand. Are you unwilling to tell me, or do you expect me to just believe you? I want to stay here, to help you, to help the town to see you as I do. But I can't do that if what they believe," he halted, knowing his words would hurt, but needing to know all the same, "is really the truth."

He swallowed hard as Seraphina spun around to face him. He wanted to see anger, to have her stomp back to him and prove him wrong, just as she'd done in the cabin with her dagger. He wanted to see the passion and light he knew was inside her. Instead, her shoulders dropped and he thought for a moment that she might fall to her knees. He took two steps forward to catch her if she did.

"Believe what you will," her words gouged him as she strode away.

CHAPTER 13

Would anyone trust her? Ever? She'd helped all she could, given to those in need, and yet no one would believe her word. Not Lenora, who had treated her as if her malady were an exaggeration, and not Geoff, not even Cort and all the others who sought out her knowledge of healing when the doctor wasn't available. When had they decided her help was the only thing good about her?

And were they right?

Seraphina slowed her pace as she neared her home. Geoff would return there to sleep soon. Since he wanted her to change her sleeping to match his own, he wouldn't stay out much later. If she wasn't there, he couldn't push her any more for answers she couldn't give. She bypassed her house and slowly angled to the river, past the jail, and near the mines. It was there she met with the few Miwak who would speak to her.

Not all of the bands were connected, and some kept

their distance from her. The Miwak were tribal and many small groups lived in the area. The largest had moved farther up the mountain away from the river, but it was replaced by smaller ones. Some were friendly, others were not. She watched carefully on the other side of the river for the stoic faces to appear. They could manage to stand near the river, perfectly still, and in the dark became almost invisible within the trees. Until she'd learned just what to look for, they had frightened her when they would suddenly move.

She stared at the rushing water and the trees, waiting. The lull of the water calmed her. Though she'd only known Geoff for a few days, she didn't want him to go and his words cut deeply. She'd thought he might be the first person to care about her in a long time. He'd reminded her of all the things she'd missed when her brother left, and much more. Her brother was never tender and kind, but Geoff was. He'd given her provisions, helped her back to her cabin, stayed with her and even walked with her. Which was more than even Lenora had done.

Was her secret so burdensome that it couldn't be shared? Was it worth the risk? He'd planned to leave anyway. It had only been a few days since they'd met. If he left it shouldn't affect her, yet she knew it would. It had been a few wonderful days of conversation she'd craved for so long.

An owl hooted above her and its mate replied in kind. Seraphina wanted that, though she'd never put a name to it before. She wanted what *Maman* and *Père* had shared

—love. She wanted to smile when her husband came home after a long day, to kiss him then melt briefly in his arms. But she was destined to never have such a life, because unless he came home in the late evening, he would have to return to a darkened house for her to greet him.

Would any man be willing to put up with that? Geoff had only been there a few days and he was already tired of it, tired of her insistence that she must remain not only hidden but, covered. Her brother had always been exhausted after working a long day at the mines. He'd come in while she was still sleeping, had eaten what she'd left for him, done whatever chores needed to be done outside so he didn't bother her, then he'd gone to bed before she'd even arisen for the day. They had rarely spoken. That was no life for a husband. It would test him to the limit.

If Geoff couldn't live with her need to remain hidden, he may leave just as Martin had. Could she stand the abandonment? Geoff had taken over caring of every need she couldn't provide for herself as soon as he'd appeared and now dread filled her at that loss. The loss of yet another friend.

Seraphina pulled her dagger from its sheath on her thigh. Though it was dark, she could see the smudge of shadow where the crest was on the hilt. That was all she had left of her family—an image on a dagger. Didn't she owe it to herself to try for something more? Wasn't life meant to be more than sleeping and work?

The dagger meant nothing. It wouldn't bring back

Martin, it wouldn't answer her questions. It wouldn't provide much of anything without her help. It was as useless as her life if she didn't push against her fears and face them. If Geoff was so certain he needed to know her secret, then he couldn't hold it against her.

Sliding the dagger back in its place, Seraphina stood and made her way back to her cabin. By the light of the moon, it was approaching the darkest hour and Geoff would be fast asleep. She wouldn't bother him this night, but tomorrow, when he arrived back home after he left for the day, she would tell him. He had to handle what he asked for, and if not, then he wouldn't have stayed anyway.

She pushed the door open slowly and closed it behind her so it didn't squeak. The habit had fallen by the wayside when she'd come to live alone. If Geoff continued to stay in Blessings, he may stay with her until he could start his shop. The mere idea warmed a place in her heart.

No more loneliness.

The need to see him, her future if she allowed herself to be honest and tell him her secret, was too great to ignore. Seraphina lit her lamp and though she didn't approach his bed, she held the light and turned to face Geoff's bed. It was still made and his coat lay where he'd left it before they had taken their walk. He hadn't come back to the cabin.

GEOFF STARED at Seraphina's cabin as he strode into the clearing and stopped in his tracks. He'd only been there a few days, but already he felt a connection with the woman who'd been cast aside, the woman who didn't fit in, just like him. With her cape and living in darkness, she was much like him, hiding his scars and his possible heritage. Or, what he'd begun to assume was his heritage.

He'd wanted to talk to Lenora, confront her about her knowledge of their mother, because the secrets of his past must come from his mother's side. They were the people he'd never met, those who wouldn't associate with Edward Farnsworth or his offspring. They held the answers. And Lenora had known Mother better than he had, she was the key.

He'd heard the rumors back in Boston, people called his mother mulatto behind her back, had treated her as if she'd tricked his father into marriage. But was any of it true? If it was, it would explain his own darker appearance and it would explain why he'd been so abused at the hands of the privateer captain.

The captain had said *his kind* didn't bleed the same, *his kind* didn't feel the same, and he hadn't understood. Why would the lashes feel any less for him than anyone else? Now, he needed to know if the captain had been right. Though it would change nothing. He was who he was, permanently scarred by the hate of others. Seraphina had never looked on him as if he was less because his skin was a few shades darker than other men's, she didn't flinch when she looked in his eyes, and didn't stare. She'd allowed him to stay with her, but she didn't trust him.

If that trust could be built, maybe then she would share her secret with him. And if she did, then he'd have to share his with her. When she'd run off, he'd wanted her to come back. It had been a realization as sharp as a dash of cold water. He couldn't just be with her, she had to be important to him. It was her choice to trust him, but if she did, she could have his heart.

Staying in Blessings, for her, would be a start but wasn't where he wanted to ultimately be. If he wanted to stay in Blessings and take her on as a partner in his business, not only did he need to trust her, she needed honesty from him. He slid his sleeve up just slightly and felt the bumps left behind by the deep scars.

Hideous.

Even though Seraphina hid her skin, would she understand his need to hide his own? Would they come to some sort of understanding when he understood her secret? She was beautiful and had no visible reason to hide, not like him. He could only think of the people she'd encountered in the past who had shunned and hurt her. They must be part of the puzzle. They had to have provided the reason for her to hide. He'd never been ashamed of his own skin until he'd been told it wasn't worth living in.

Geoff yanked his sleeve down and strode toward town. Before he could talk to Seraphina, he had to finally talk to his sister. If she didn't have the information, his father had given him the key with the book. He didn't have to leave, the black book held an address, one he could write to. He could be in touch with them, but stay with Seraphina. His mother's family, a family he wanted to contact. It was time they became one once again.

They may not care about him, but he'd at least give them the chance to shun him. It was more than he'd given his father and Lenora before he'd run off. Hopefully, when given the truth, Seraphina wouldn't make that same choice.

CHAPTER 14

The evening had grown thick into full night and the home his father had told him was Victor and Lenora's was dark as Geoff strode up the street. There was no movement in the little town, only the music and laughter from the saloon. Though there were people there, they were most likely not the ones he needed the most.

Yet, how long had he gone without a drink, or a hand of cards? He thought back to that fateful day he'd been found in the alley. It had been months before and he'd been dry ever since. Tonight, when weariness ate at him like a dog on a bone, the bottle and the tables called.

He wasn't a drunk, at least he could claim that. He didn't drink every day, certainly didn't need to now, but why should he be forced to stay away? No one would know him there. It wasn't like his father or Lenora would hear about it. Even Victor, who'd loved a drink now and again, never went to the saloon. Lenora hadn't cared that he'd been minding himself since he walked into town. She hadn't bothered to let him in yet.

He made his way down the street, letting the light of the front windows be his guide. When he'd been in Blessings before, the saloon had been a hastily built structure, with a slight lean, like it might tip over at any moment. Now, it had been repaired into a sizable building, taking up a full third of the street. While it was still Ellie's, and he'd spent a fair number of hours inside before he'd run, it was completely foreign to him.

Ellie stood behind the bar, her brash red hair the first noticeable thing in the building. She nodded to him and finished pouring a drink, then glanced back up at him and waved him over.

He made it to the bar and slung himself over a stool, the familiar bar seating too comfortable to him.

"I'd heard you were back in town and wondered when you'd come to visit. Didn't hardly recognize you." Ellie wiped out a glass.

He rested his hands on the old bar, solid as oak. "I didn't think you'd remember me."

"And just why wouldn't I? You practically lived here for about two weeks before you disappeared."

He'd even asked her if he could bed down under the bar, because he hadn't wanted to go home to face his father. Being homeless had been preferable to letting his father down, which had finally led him to leave. "Still, it's been years. You've changed the place."

Ellie laughed slightly. "I guess the changes happened so slowly, I just don't think about them

116

anymore. It all seems business as usual now. Can I get you anything?"

A drink. He took a long, deep breath and his lungs filled with the cheroot smoke lingering in the room. Ellie's could have been any number of other saloons in California—most were the same, no matter what little town he'd been in. The only difference was, some places watered down the spirits so much a man had to practically drown himself to feel good. He'd tried.

"I'll take whatever you've got there." He nodded to the bottle still in front of her. It didn't matter what it was, he'd tried just about everything to make his mother's voice leave him be.

He sat up straighter on his stool when he realized the absence. He hadn't heard her since he'd found Seraphina. His mother's pestering him to come home and bring the family back together, was silent.

Ellie set the drink in front of him and he dug in his pocket for his two bits to pay for it. When she left, he stared down at the amber liquid in the tall mug. How would Seraphina feel about him avoiding her to go to the saloon? Would his *maman* really want him there? Would his father sigh with disapproval? Would being there help him make Lenora see he'd changed? Wasn't he falling right back into his old trap? He pushed the drink away and stood.

The problem was, it was now the middle of the night. He couldn't talk to his family without waking them all up and he couldn't go back to Seraphina's until he had a clear idea of who he was because she deserved that. A man was no man if he didn't even know what he stood for.

The music and lively stomping from the back drew him. It was the one thing about Ellie's that wasn't like every other place in California, and hadn't been like that when he'd left. There were also no sporting women, not that he was in a sporting mood. He stood in the doorway and stared over the quickly spinning and twirling couples on the floor. A man stood off to the side and nudged him.

"You want to pay for a dance?"

He hadn't done anything like it since he'd left Boston and he'd been young then, full of ideas about the ladies at the parties his mother and father had made him attend. The ladies of the hall were nothing like those women. Though they didn't offer anything except a dance, it was with the intent to fill a man's need to be near a woman, unlike the parties he'd been to, where a dance might lead to connections, and then relationships. Those parties were all business wrapped in the mask of fun and costly appearances.

"One," Geoff mumbled. Perhaps the brief time with another woman would stop his rampant thoughts of a French maiden wandering around the forests of Blessings. The very maiden who wouldn't give up her secrets to him. The one who'd captured his mind and wouldn't let go. Though she be slight, her hold on him was fast.

The music came to an end and the couples separated. The man next to him pointed to each woman and a man along the wall who raised his hand. The woman would approach that man and lead him to the dancefloor. Geoff watched the whole proceeding so intently, he almost missed the dark-haired woman who curtsied in front of him. She held out her hand and he took it, letting her lead him to the middle of the floor.

"What is your name?" he asked her. Her eyes were dark, like his own.

"What would you like it to be?" she responded, closing her eyes as she let him lead them to the music.

He searched the woman's face, and though he couldn't find a fault or flaw, she wasn't the pretty dark-haired beauty he wanted to dance with. His beauty had porcelain skin and wore a flower behind her ear, her eyes gleamed in the lamplight, golden like a cat's. His beauty needed him to finish his job so he could learn how to make boots and provide for her.

He stopped the dance a few moments after it started and stepped away from her. The woman glanced over to the man at the door, her eyes wide. "Have I done something to make you unhappy?"

He shook his head, but his heart knew what it wanted. He didn't have to worry about the girl if he left the dance, she would still earn her pay. He simply couldn't continue when she wasn't the woman he wanted to hold. "No, it's just that my arms want to hold another woman, not any women here. I'm sorry." He tipped his hat and turned for the door.

The man sent him a quizzical glance. "Something wrong?"

"Not with her. I just lost my footing is all."

There was nothing he could do there that would help him, nothing that would make him think clearer or help him find answers. But proving to his family that he was willing to work hard to make his own way, those were things he could do.

He'd planned to ask his father and Mr. Winslet to help him start up his shop, but that would just prove to them he still needed help. If he helped himself, made his own money to start up the boot shop, then he might prove them wrong. Once he proved them wrong, they might be more willing to listen and then he could talk to Lenora.

Ellie waved him back to the bar, but he just nodded her way and headed for the door. If he hurried, he might be able to catch Cort at the livery. He'd always been a nocturnal person, the one who used to watch the gambling tent late into the night and sometimes early morning. Cort had probably witnessed Seraphina more than anyone else in town, besides himself.

The livery sat just down the road from Victor's house and there was a newer home just behind it with one lamp sitting in a window by the door, waiting for someone. Cort hadn't left yet. The livery still smelled more like new wood than horse droppings and he glanced at the newly completed back corner. They'd worked all day, getting everything repaired. The loft could be used. Geoff strode over to the door and slid it open slightly. It was a long wide barn with stalls on either side. His horse with no name stood in the end stall.

"Who goes there?" Cort called from the back of the building.

"Cort, it's Geoff." He slid all the way into the building and pulled the door closed behind him.

"I didn't think I'd ever see you again after the repairs were completed. Victor wasn't easy to work with."

Geoff had been young and stupid when he'd left Blessings and had said some things to Cort he regretted. He'd accused both Victor and Cort of being dishonest. They hadn't talked about that day, but if he was going to really work for Cort, they needed to clear the air. Hat in hand, he approached the livery owner and prayed he would forget the past and help him.

"I've come back to Blessings to make things right with my family. And others." He swallowed hard. "I accused you of dishonesty."

"It's water under the bridge, Geoff. You helped when we needed you and you were more right than you could know at the time, anyway. Are you here to pay for that horse? I didn't believe Atherton when he told me it was yours. I was ready to just assume it was mine if no one showed up to get it. Glad you let me know earlier, Hannah has taken a shine to it."

He chuckled. If he didn't need that horse to go get hides, he'd sell it to Cort. "Need any help tonight? Maybe I could bed down up in the loft?"

Cort stared at him as he reached behind the stove for the broom. "You know you're welcome as long as you're willing to work. Told you as much yesterday. But, I'd heard you were staying with Seraphina. Thought we could finally be done worrying about her."

They all had a strange way of worrying about

Seraphina. Not a one had cared. Geoff stomped forward, his blood boiling in his veins as he clenched his fists. The whole town needed fixing and it would start with Cort. "And just why would you need to worry about Seraphina? Were you worried she'd hex you?"

Cort took a deep breath and shoved him down onto the nearest stool, then took his seat once again. "No, you fool. Hannah and I have worried about her alone out in that cabin since her brother left. We've tried leaving things for her by her door, because she doesn't answer during the day at all anymore and people sure do talk if you're seen by her place at night, but I think people must take them before she gets them."

"You leave her things?" Had he misunderstood the feeling of the whole town about Seraphina?

"Yes. She helped me a few years ago, right about the time her brother disappeared, and I never forgot her. She helped Hannah too. We've even met at the church with some of the people of Blessings, to see if there's anything we can do. Problem is, we had been sending things with Lenora but Victor won't let Lenora go there now. Seraphina won't go near anyone and, if she hears people coming, she dashes off into the trees. I'll be boggled if she doesn't see better than anyone I know in the dark."

"She doesn't know." Geoff raked his hand through his hair but that only frustrated him more. If the town could let her know she was welcome, then she wouldn't need him. She would be free of him and his scars. He could focus on his family and not burden the woman who'd stolen his heart with his own needs. "I've talked to Victor and he has no love for Seraphina. He can't be the only one. Her fear has to come from somewhere."

Cort shook his head and glanced over Geoff's shoulder to the horses behind him. "Victor is terrified of anything he can't control. It's his biggest fault and always has been. He may have changed quite a bit to become a man your sister could love, but he never changed who he was completely. As to the town, some folks believe what they will."

"That doesn't make sense. No man can be controlled." Not even by force, because it wouldn't change a man's desires.

"Victor is worried that if the few people who still think Seraphina is a witch are right, then something could happen to the few things he has that matter to him, Lenora and his child."

He couldn't let Victor stand in his way. Seraphina deserved to be free. "But there's still hope? The town could convince her to come out, to show her face and be a part of the community."

Cort clenched his jaw and pushed against his knees to stand. "It's not that easy. Most want to welcome her, but there are a few vocal citizens who would rather she stay right where she is. Atherton has worried about inviting her out, just to be mocked and heckled by those few loud people, all of us have, not because we care about them, but because of the damage it could do to her. It could make her hide forever, or worse, leave."

Geoff would gladly take her with him if she would

consider it. "Why would leaving be so horrible if there are people who don't want her here?"

Cort moved slowly to the desk in the corner and slid papers into the one drawer. "Because if she leaves, Atherton can't keep an eye on her. He feels a bit like a father to her, she reminds him of one of his own. One he hasn't seen in quite a long time." Cort turned down the lamp on the desk, leaving only the lanterns hanging by the stalls. "Sweep up a bit down here, then you're welcome to the cot up in the loft. We'll talk tomorrow about any other work you can do and how long you'll be here."

He prayed it wasn't long. His mother's, and his, goal of making the family whole could start right there in that livery. Once he was sure of who he was after talking to Lenora, he could return to Seraphina and beg for her trust. And more. If only he'd been blessed with patience.

CHAPTER 15

I t had never been a struggle to keep herself busy. Seraphina had always managed to make use of her time with reading, making her tinctures, salves, and poultices, sewing or any number of things, but with the absence of Geoff, all those things were less important. After just a few days, he'd come to be a part of her house and his empty bed taunted her. She was too *odd* for him. Even though she'd told him she wasn't a witch, it hadn't been enough. He believed she was.

With little effort, Seraphina poured the last of her whiskey into a pot sitting on the back of the stove. It had to slowly steep through the day, so she couldn't let it get too hot. Though the work had to get done so she could help her bruises heal, it wouldn't help her bruised pride. He'd offered to stay with her, had even *pushed* to stay, then had walked away once she was used to the idea of having him around. He'd left as soon as she'd decided she would miss him.

The glass bottles on her shelves vibrated and clinked together and two of them fell and shattered. She ran to the wall and tried to hold them in place as her walls shook with vibrations coming up from the floor. This wasn't the first time it had happened since she'd lived there. One had been so violent, she'd lost almost all of her medicines.

One bottle fell from a high shelf and hit the side of her head. The alcohol burned her eyes and she screamed, immediately blinded by the liquid. She backed from the falling glass and slammed into the table. Seraphina couldn't keep her footing with the swaying of the floor and fell to her knees. A warm trickle ran down the side of her face that could have been tincture or blood, there was no way to tell. She touched the spot above her eye where she'd been hit and prayed she would remain conscious long enough to clean up.

She hadn't seen which bottle had hit her, but it continued to burn her as she searched by touch along the floor for her wash pail. It wasn't antiseptic, but at least she could remove whatever had hit her.

Outside, people screamed into the night as they ran from house to house, checking on other families. Men rushed by her cabin, calling for wives or asking about animals that had escaped. She listened, focusing on the voices, wanting nothing more than for Geoff to come and find her, to worry about her, to help her. Hadn't he said he would look after her? After a few minutes, she gave up listening and went back to her search for her bucket to clean herself up. He wasn't coming back.

Abandonment stung worse than the gash in her head. Hadn't he said he was going to look after her until she healed? Yet, he hadn't asked about her wounds since that day. He may have thought that since she was well enough to go out gathering, she was well enough to live on her own once again. Alone. He hadn't even warned her he wasn't coming back, just like Martin.

Her fingers located the metal pail she kept in the back corner for cleaning, and the washrag hung over the edge. It was damp from wiping off the table earlier, but blinded, she didn't have any choice but to use what was available. At least it was only water in the bucket and the only time she'd dipped anything in it, had been the clean rag.

Seraphina dipped the cloth back into the water and gently dabbed and washed away the debris of the tincture along with the alcohol. Once her eyes were clear, she was able to find a clean cloth and made quick work of cleaning the gashes on the side of her head. At least she hadn't found any glass shards still in her skin.

Soft morning light invaded her windows and Seraphina covered them. She slipped on her cape and gloves. Since Geoff hadn't returned to sleep, it was possible he was still outside, and caught in the earthquake. If he was hurt, he *couldn't* return. She had to believe it, had to believe he was hurt rather than avoiding her.

Ducking outside her door, she ignored the people rushing about. They paid her no heed as they scurried around. Some of the weaker small homes around her own were little more than heaps of ruin. People ran around frantically or seemed to be in a daze. All had such focus, they didn't notice her. Seraphina ducked farther into the woods and headed along the trail to the clearing where Geoff found her the evening before.

All along the way, she could hear the sounds of people. The higher the sun rose, the more she hunched to keep all light from touching her, but she couldn't see well, not much more than a few feet beyond her hems. It terrified her to hold her head up to search around. Seraphina held the hood of her cape out like an awning, so she could see farther over the clearing. Geoff wasn't there, and it was far enough away from the town she could no longer hear the people.

Had he rushed back into town to check on his family? That would be an easy way to let them know he cared about them. Seraphina slowly made her way to Winslet House. It didn't have any structural damage and she kept moving, staying by trees and buildings, until she reached main street.

None of the buildings along Main Street were damaged, though people stood outside, talking and pointing. Those who had lived there longest knew that there was never just one earthquake, it was always followed by more. It was best not to be inside where a body could get crushed.

Mr. Farnsworth stood outside with Atherton and Ed from the mercantile, but Geoff wasn't anywhere along the street. The morning grew hotter as the sun rose, and Seraphina wanted to duck back into her house, away from it. Even avoiding its rays, fully covered, she could feel the prickle of heat in her skin and the unbearable itch clawed its way to the surface.

She would check Lenora's, then rush back home. She couldn't be caught outside when her skin erupted in hives and rash or she would never be able to dispel the false notion that she was a witch. There were still long shadows along the side of the building as she rushed toward the Abernathy home.

Victor would never allow her inside. Lenora had told Seraphina that her husband would not relent in his distrust of her. No matter how Lenora begged. She couldn't risk going to the door, but if Lenora was outside, Geoff might be as well. When she got close enough, she could see Lenora, Hannah, Cort, and Victor all outside, pointing to a bit of damage on the corner of the Abernathy home. Some rock had shifted out from the foundation and would need to be repaired.

Geoff wasn't there.

With a last glance up and down the street, Seraphina made her way back to her cabin and closed the door. Once inside, she removed her cape and gloves, allowing her skin to breathe. She went to the washstand and dripped cool water over her arms and face where the prickling always started.

Fatigue made her wobble, she hadn't eaten all night and now the day had come. If she added wood to the stove, it would get too hot for her to sleep and would hurt her tincture. There was no reason to worry about the tincture for her shoulder and wrist anymore, not when it appeared that Geoff had left Blessings. Her heart already ached more with his disappearance than her shoulder.

If she'd only given up her secret, he might still be there. If only she'd allowed herself to trust. He hadn't asked for much, yet she'd denied him just as his family had. He'd told her she was the only reason he was staying in Blessings until Lenora would speak to him, yet she'd forgotten that when it was important.

Seraphina gathered her soft cape and curled it under her head. The compress on her wound felt damp, but she didn't have the heart or energy to clean and re-dress it. Geoff was gone. Forever gone. The Farnsworths had seemed like the only family who cared about her, but they were also quick to give up on her, and break her heart. She would never have family again.

Her tears soaked her cloak and the damp fabric cooled her heated cheeks. She had stayed in Blessings hoping her brother would return and that Lenora would eventually come back. Now, she'd waited long enough. Geoff had stayed because of her, but without him, there was no longer a reason to remain. Blessings would be better without her.

There had to be a way to return to France if she wasn't welcome anywhere else. She had the money from Martin's last pay. She clutched the blade on her outer thigh through her skirt and petticoats. Someone would know how to find her family. There had to be somewhere in the world she would be accepted, maybe even loved. There had to be somewhere to call home.

CHAPTER 16

There was dust floating through the air and Geoff's nose and throat burned with it. Everyone in the entire town seemed to be standing around with little to do but talk. He swiped the sweat from his brow and pushed the broom a little harder.

Cort strode up to him, his expression grim. "I don't see any damage. Rough night."

Geoff leaned against the broom, glad for a moment's break. "Rough? What happened?" He'd been so exhausted from staying up for a day and a half that he'd slept hard straight through the night.

"You didn't feel the earthquake?" Cort asked him, looking surprised. "You're lucky you didn't get shaken right out of bed."

With the cot he'd been in, it would've swayed him a bit, but Geoff hadn't noticed. "Seraphina." He rushed to the door and glanced up the hill, but he couldn't see her little hidden cabin from there.

"Your family are all fine," Cort mumbled. "In case you were worried."

He should've asked about them first, but they hadn't been his primary thought. "I'm glad." He turned and faced a solemn-faced Cort. "But as you said last night, someone needs to worry about Seraphina."

Cort nodded, but gave no clue how he really felt. "Victor has some damage, but it can be repaired. He won't be here today so he can see to it."

At least he wouldn't have to deal with Victor and obviously Lenora was fine since Cort had said so. "Mind if I go check on her?" No one else would. If she were hurt, she would sit there all day. If something fell and hit her, she could be injured.

"Atherton accounted for everyone in town. I already asked. This quake was pretty minor. Mostly shanties were damaged, and the Abernathy's. I hired you to work here, so I'd appreciate it if you'd put in your day."

He closed his eyes and prayed Seraphina was all right. He should've gone back to her cabin instead of being bull-headed about her secret and his own. Keeping himself from her wasn't going to make her trust him more, it would make her trust him *less*.

"I would only be a few minutes."

Cort shook his head. "The work is on the list posted on my desk. I've got my own things that need tending. Get the work done, then you can go run off where you need to. Don't get the work done and you don't have a job."

Cort had given him work, even knowing Victor wouldn't approve. He'd trusted Geoff even though he hadn't been trustworthy before he'd left Blessings. If he dashed out now, it would break that trust and he might not find work elsewhere, nor could he ever find more perfect work for Lenora to hear about it. Working for the livery where her husband was half owner was about the best job he could ask for. Yet, he desperately wanted to check on Seraphina.

Everyone was accounted for.

Atherton knew Seraphina, cared about her like family, he'd told Geoff where to find her and had given her the envelope full of money. He wouldn't neglect Seraphina now. Geoff strode over to the desk and checked the list. It was long and would take him most of the day, especially if he wanted to get the jobs done right. He peered out at the blue sky. She would be sleeping, he had to trust she'd been accounted for and was now resting like usual.

Victor strode toward the livery around noon time and watched Geoff work for a few minutes, then added to Cort's long list.

He crossed his arms and stood nearby. "Your sister is well, even with the damage to her home."

Geoff didn't bother to look up, that would only add to Victor's ire. "Yes, Cort told me right away this morning. I stayed away, since she had enough to bother her without me and Cort would rather I stay here." He pitched the used hay behind him, his eyes watering from the smell and dust. He'd never been a horseman. In Boston, there had been no need. When he'd lived along the coast of California, he'd taken stages when he'd wanted to move to the next town. The work—and smell—was more than he was used to. At least he had more clothes now from his father. Clothes that were back with Seraphina.

"So, you do have a head on your shoulders and think about people other than yourself. There's hope for you yet." Victor turned and left the barn, giving Geoff a moment to catch his breath.

As soon as he'd finished his work, he dashed from the barn and ran up the hill. It was still full daylight outside, since summer left the days long and hot. He reached her door, panting and sweating with the exertion. If she wasn't hurt, she'd be sleeping, and he hoped she was. He wanted to talk to her, even if it meant staying up with her, but he needed to clean up so he could stand to breathe. He'd check on her first, then head to the river for a scrub.

Geoff gently pushed the door open, ducked inside, and closed it behind him. The complete darkness took over and his eyes flashed the reflection of the bright outdoors for a moment. Seraphina whimpered from her bed to his left. He made his way to her, and found the lamp by her bed. He lit it and set the lamp back down. The side of her head was covered in a bandage that was deep red, and her cheeks held red streaks from tears she'd shed in her sleep.

He gently removed the gory bandage to reveal a deep red slash on her temple. He'd seen enough of his own wounds to know she needed to be seen by someone more knowledgeable than himself and he knew better than to touch it with his hands, which were filthy from the livery.

He couldn't leave her without saying something, in case she was waking from the lantern. "I'll go get some help, Seraphina." He wanted to kiss her tenderly, let her know he'd take care of her, but not in his state. He rushed from the little cabin and headed for Dr. Edwards.

When he reached the hospital, he found the doctor was flooded with minor injuries from the earthquake, mostly cuts and sprains. He couldn't leave his patients to come check on Seraphina and Geoff couldn't move her all the way to the hospital without help. That left one person—Lenora. He'd have to face her in order to help Seraphina.

If Seraphina had been bleeding like that since the earthquake, hours earlier, she could be too weakened to move on her own. He should've been there. He should've left work to check. Geoff scolded himself as he rushed for the Abernathy house. He reached their door and pounded on it, tired and needing to find help.

Victor answered and scowled at him from the doorway. "What in the name of all that's good are you doing here?"

He wanted to push right past Victor and into the house to find Lenora. She wouldn't be able to say no to someone in need. "I need Lenora."

"Well, she doesn't need you. She is laying down now. The doctor said she's had enough for one day and now she needs to rest."

No. Seraphina needed help. More than he could offer. "It's Seraphina. She was hurt in the earthquake and the doctor is too busy. Please."

Lenora poked her head around from the hall. "What's going on?" Her deep blue eyes reminded him of Father's when he was younger. At least now they weren't snapping at him.

"She has a gash on her head. I need your help, please." It wasn't really a question, but he'd be polite.

Lenora gripped her slightly rounded waist. "I've worried about her. I was sure she was fine, since she's such a strong woman. I'll grab my shawl."

Victor puffed out his chest. "You don't need to go over there. You know how I feel about that woman."

"And you know how I feel about you. I love you, despite your stubborn ways. I listen to you because I do love you. But Seraphina needs me." Lenora rushed back through and passed her husband. "At some point you'll realize I sometimes choose to be friends with people who aren't reputable and well-liked."

Geoff held in a laugh to keep Victor from turning on him yet again. Victor had been about as disreputable as a man could get before he'd changed so he could be worthy of Lenora. Victor slammed his jaw closed with a loud *clack* and Geoff held the door for Lenora.

Once they were away from the house, Lenora slowed her pace and glanced over her shoulder at him. For a moment, it was years before and there were no angry words or animosity between them.

"Why me?" she mumbled, holding her skirts out of the dust while she waited for him to catch up.

"You were the only one I could think of. I went to the doctor first, worried you wouldn't even let me in your house. When he was too busy, I had to risk it. We can't just leave her there."

"Atherton said he'd checked everyone." She headed for the narrow street that led up the hill, then peaked at the river's edge.

"I'm sure he did, but her cabin had no exterior damage and he wouldn't just go inside if she didn't let him in."

"I'm surprised he didn't come to get me. He knows she and I were—" Lenora let the words hang. While he'd never let his sister's drive to be a lawyer in place of him cloud his feelings for her, he couldn't let the way she'd treated Seraphina pass.

"Friends? Is that what you call it when you take the time to learn about another person, then leave them for no good reason?" Though his words bit his own hide. He'd also left Seraphina and his own family without returning or explaining. He should've told her his plan, told her he had to do what he'd come to Blessings to do before he returned for her, because he would return.

"You don't understand, Geoff. Victor won't see reason where Seraphina is concerned and he is my husband. He has spent so much time with the miners and workers in Blessings, he's never fit in well with Atherton or anyone else, really. Even he and Father don't always see eye-to-eye. So, when he hears all these things about the witch, even words from his wife and his closest friend won't dissuade him."

"She's alone, Lenora. Why didn't you try to change what people think of her?" Why hadn't he done the same? Was he so caught up in the secret she kept that he wasn't willing to do what was right? He'd been given the opportunity to be what Miss Rosa had been for him, only he'd let Seraphina float by, instead of pulling her out of the water.

"Yes, she is alone. She has other maladies that keep her there. Not many would even be willing to do as I did by visiting her at night."

He rushed ahead a few steps until he was abreast of Lenora. "You know why? What keeps her inside?"

Lenora glanced at him, her eyes holding back more than worry. "I do, but that's for her to tell, not me. It's almost too much to believe if you would hear it from anyone but her. Which is why I haven't told anyone, especially my husband, who would take her malady as proof of what he believes to be true." Lenora stopped by Seraphina's door and knocked lightly, then slowly pushed the door open. Geoff followed her inside.

Seraphina lay just where he'd left her, and Lenora knelt beside the bed. She was hardly showing any signs of pregnancy and her movements were comfortable, as if she'd been there often.

"For how long have you slipped away to visit Seraphina?" He stopped by the door. He had no help to offer.

"Not now, Geoff." Lenora touched lightly around

Seraphina's head wound. "The gash is fairly clean, whatever hit her was sharp. But there's oil and debris still making a mess of it. She never would've left anyone else like this."

He approached the bed, knowing it wasn't his place but needing to offer some kind of help. "Her eyes are very red, too."

Lenora scowled at him, then quickly stood to her full height. She was fairly diminutive, but with the fire in her eyes, she was the strength of women, directed right at him. "Since her cloak is soaked, I assumed the redness was from her tears."

She had returned to find her home empty, and probably expected him to be there. After their brief argument, he should've come back to make it right. But he'd been tired after staying up so many hours and worried he'd start a real fight. If he'd said the wrong thing, it would've only made it worse. But was he justifying his actions, just as he'd done for years after leaving Blessings?

Lenora turned and headed for the stove, then stopped dead in her tracks. "Geoff...look." She pointed to the wall of tinctures.

He'd come in and been focused completely on Seraphina. The outside of her home had no damage, so he'd only thought of her. But the wall was a mess of shifted and broken bottles. It was like his nose became aware of the mess as soon as he saw it. The pungent scent of alcohol and fermenting vegetation lingered in the air.

"I think I know what cut her." Lenora moved steadily to the wall and righted one bottle leaning precariously against another. "It will take her years to replace all of those bottles," Lenora mumbled. "I wish I knew how to help."

"Why does she bother making so much?" She couldn't possibly use all of those on her own.

Lenora took a deep breath, then left the wall and continued her way to the stove. She knelt beside it and flipped through some rags laying in a box. "She does it because many people in this town trust her medicines. They are cheaper than the salesmen who travel between the towns and it saves the doctor from trying to provide for everyone. He has even sent people to find her. The fact that they have to come after dark puts some off, but not all."

She found a few rags, then grabbed a bag he'd never seen before behind Seraphina's food storage box. It looked like a medical bag.

"What is that?" He came closer, sure he couldn't be seeing what was right in front of him.

"It's a medical bag. She doesn't bring it out often, only when people are very hurt. She hurt herself badly on the way to Blessings and had to stay with a kind doctor in Coloma. She and her brother stayed so long that he helped her learn things, like stitching up wounds, and making tinctures. Since Blessings has a doctor, she doesn't feel like she should use what she learned."

"Hurt herself?" How little he knew about Seraphina, but how could he after just a few days? It was like his heart knew her better than his own mind.

"It isn't my story to tell."

He growled at his sister's unwillingness to help him understand. "And just how am I supposed to find anything out about this woman if you won't help me?"

"Ask." Seraphina's voice drifted from across the room and they both whipped around. It was like being caught where he shouldn't be, even though he'd been staying there.

Geoff strode quickly to her bed and pulled up a chair from the table. He sat down, ready to ask all that he'd been wondering, but he'd already tried that. She had refused to give up her secrets just the night before. Asking had yielded nothing but a fight.

Lenora brought over a brown bottle and the rags. "You can talk later. For now, I must get this cleaned up and wrapped. Geoff, you can help or leave, but I won't have you sitting there staring. It might be best if you go wash yourself up." With a slight push, she shoved him off the chair and out of her way.

He moved and sat on the bed, reaching for Seraphina's hands. "What can I do?"

Seraphina gave him a wistful smile. "Listen," she muttered then flinched as Lenora cleaned her wound.

If that was all she required of him for now, that's exactly what he would do.

CHAPTER 17

The smell of frying bacon made Seraphina's stomach grumble in readiness. If Geoff heard the noise from his station by the stove, he made no move to let her know. Gingerly, she touched the bandaged area at her temple and forced herself to deal with the sharp pain.

Lenora had done well in bandaging her up, but then she'd left without speaking to Seraphina or Geoff. He'd gone over to the stove and started cooking almost as soon as the door had closed. Seraphina couldn't help but assume he was hurt by his sister's refusal to talk. Lenora had been mum the entire time Seraphina was awake, not even bothering to explain why she'd suddenly disappeared, or reappeared, nor if her reappearance was permanent.

"You're home?" She flinched slightly, but Geoff didn't turn to see it. She should have said, "you've returned". That would've been more truthful. He wasn't home.

Geoff took a minute to turn all the slices of bacon in the pan before he answered. "I'm back for a bit tonight, to make sure you're all right. I have a job down at the livery and they need me to stay there. So, I'll be heading back over in a bit. Don't worry. I'll be here every night to check on you." He smiled slightly, but something was off. He wasn't acting assertive, as he had since he'd arrived.

"I'm glad you've found work, but what about your boot shop?" She'd planned to learn right alongside him and help, but if he didn't need her, then her place was right there in her cabin. Safe, alone, until she could plan her trip back to France. He'd returned, but he'd yet to act as he had before, as if he wanted to be there with her.

"I may need more money to start it than I've saved. It's a good way to show my father and Lenora that I plan to stay in Blessings and be a part of the town."

Lenora had said her husband had felt the same way, and so had started the livery with Cort. It worked. The people of Blessings now respected him.

"Why was Lenora here?" When she'd been woken by the prodding, she'd been surprised to find her old friend with her. Seeing Geoff had made her too happy to even think about asking, but now she wanted to know.

"I asked her to come and help. I don't know the first thing about wounds or doctoring. The doctor had so many patients after the earthquake, I couldn't ask him to leave, so I went to get Lenora. She did come, but we still haven't talked."

He pushed the pan to the back of the stove and came to her bed, then sat down in the chair Lenora had left. He'd washed his hands, face, and neck in her wash pail, but his clothing was still dusty from the livery. He'd stayed with her the whole time Lenora had tended her wounds. Seraphina's heart raced at the worry in his eyes.

"I'll get you something to eat and sit here with you, then I should go back. I'm here to listen, just like you asked. Whenever you need."

She had asked that, but the thought was still terrifying. With his move to the livery, she wouldn't see him much at all and telling him might not matter. If he understood, he might change his mind and run.

Seraphina reached for his hand and he gladly offered it to her. She'd prayed so often for contact, for the warmth of touch. His hands were rough, unlike her own. Hers were smooth from the constant cover of her gloves. Her skin was so pale next to his. "Please promise me you will not run when I tell you."

She'd only told Lenora before. Her parents had told her she had the skin condition passed down by some in her family. The doctor who had helped her in Coloma was the first to put a name to what she had, he called it *sun sensitive*. It wasn't common, but the doctor had told her there were some people testing a treatment using sulphur in other areas of the country. She hadn't been interested in that so much as she was in knowing there were others like her. Martin had wanted to give up on California and find what he was sure would be a cure to all their problems. She'd refused to let him change his plans for her.

"I told you I would listen. I'm here." Geoff smiled at her, encouraging her to continue. He'd disappeared, hadn't mentioned their argument since his return, and had decided to find a job all in the span of a day, and though she could feel a change in him, he was still the same.

"Some people get burned in the sun and they turn temporarily dark." She held her hand up next to his and pointed to his own beautiful skin. "Some people turn red, and sore." She let their hands fall back to her lap. "But I burn horribly, a red awful rash that lasts as long as a few weeks, with blistering. It doesn't heal without the right salves and it happens after just moments in the sun. You saw just the beginning of it that very first morning you were here."

He cocked his head slightly and narrowed his eyes. "You hide, because you sunburn easily?"

She sighed and held his hand tighter. His sister hadn't understood at first, either. Perhaps she still didn't. Her skin didn't burn, it erupted. It was as if the sun were a hundred bees landing on her. "It is much worse than just a burn. It is enough that if anyone saw it, they would be terrified of me."

He nodded slowly, his eyes never leaving hers. "You're worried that if someone sees you burn, they will think the worst of you."

She let loose a heavy breath, like releasing a stone in her chest. How long had she been holding it in? "Yes, that's it exactly. No one understands that I can't go outside in the sunlight."

He lifted the damp cape from behind her where she'd lain on it. "But I saw you out in the evening light. Must you be covered all the time?"

She closed her eyes, grateful that he didn't immediately discount her ailment. "Once the sun has set, even though there is still some light, I can remove my hood safely. However, I usually wear it even at night in case I'm caught outside later than planned."

He nodded thoughtfully. "I think it's time you put this cape to better use. Go out in the day. Wear your gloves. Make the people of Blessings see you and see that you are just a person like everyone else." He touched her cheek, so gently she wanted to cry. No one had showed her such tenderness in so very long, her soul was starved for it. But he asked so much of her. If her hood slipped even slightly, it would be terrible for her.

"Come see me at work tomorrow. Sleep tonight, since you're hurt and need to heal, then take a short walk to see me at the livery. Please? Test yourself, see if the people of Blessings don't surprise you."

Only Lenora had asked her to come out during the light of day, and only once. She'd done it for her friend. She could do it for Geoff.

"I don't know that my family will ever truly accept me. My father has tried, but Lenora may never forgive me. I need family like I need air to breathe."

She waited for him to finish, but he didn't. He had family, she didn't. Seraphina didn't know how to comfort him, nor could she be that family he desired until he wanted that from her. If he ever asked that of her, she would be glad of the chance. They both had no one but each other.

"She will relent and forgive. It is her way. You just have to give her time." Seraphina let him stand and head back to the stove. Her stomach remembered she hadn't eaten in a long time and it protested again.

Geoff handed her a plate of bacon and toasted bread with butter and sat back down in his chair, balancing his plate on his lap. He offered a blessing and then started in on the small meal without providing other talk.

She wanted to tell him more, to share about her other troubles and have him understand her. If he was willing. He'd listened and tried with her biggest secret, the rest would be easier. Wasn't that just what she'd wanted, prayed for, begged of her brother? Had that been too much to ask of family, and if so, how was it that an almost stranger could take her secret and hold it better?

She smiled at him as she lifted the bacon to her lips. Though she'd been certain after Lenora left she would be alone forever, she could now see an end to the long path of loneliness she'd thought her life had become.

"I'll do as you ask. Tomorrow, I'll visit the sun."

CHAPTER 18

Cort sat outside the livery on a stool, whittling a small hunk of wood as Geoff approached. Geoff had stayed with Seraphina for as long as he dared, knowing Cort and Victor expected him to stay at the livery. Cort glanced up in the dim light and set the wood aside.

"I'm a little surprised I didn't see you come from town. Didn't you go in to check on your father?"

He'd savored every last second with Seraphina he could and hadn't even thought about anyone else once his sister had left. "Atherton said everyone was fine."

"Yet, you didn't believe that when it came to Seraphina." Cort stood and pulled his vest down over his waistband.

"I'm sure Atherton had someone check on her, it isn't him I don't trust. I'm sure he checked on my father himself. They've been friends for years."

"True. I'll use this to prove my point. I'm coming at

this caring about Seraphina's welfare, but you can't help her if you keep doing what you're doing. If you continue to keep time with her, people in Blessings might not ever come to trust you. It isn't that I feel the same as others. I've been to see Seraphina. I know there's nothing wrong with her other than that she can scare the tar out of you when you meet her wandering around at night. But others in town won't see it that way."

"What are you saying?" He'd heard so many different stories now, it was no wonder Seraphina felt trapped. He couldn't do right, no matter what he chose. Stay with her or stay away, someone was going to be angry about it.

"I'm saying, Atherton would've asked someone to go knock on her door. I doubt they ever did. If you don't stop going to that cabin, you will never build that trust you're hankering for from everyone else. You have to make a choice, build trust with her or the town. You can't do both."

He clenched his fist as the plan he'd formed slipped further from his grasp. "My family has no issue with Seraphina."

"Don't they?" Cort laughed. "Lenora used to go see her almost every day. Now, she doesn't because her husband hates Seraphina. I can't figure that out, no matter what I try. Your father has never so much as walked out there and he's lived here five whole years. That's a long time to live in a tiny little mining town and never meet someone you have no issue with."

Cort leaned more weight on one hip as he went on. "The minute your father moved from the hill down to the street, he's never looked back. He might call what people believe about Seraphina 'nonsense', but he also isn't willing to find out on his own. He used to preach *love thy neighbor* on Sunday morning, but that don't extend up the hill."

Geoff balled his fist, but punching Cort—assuming he even got close—wouldn't fix the fact that he was pitching truth. Father had never treated anyone he'd come in contact with differently because of what they looked like, but he'd never gone out of his way to find them, either. "If you have no issue with her, why don't you be the start?"

He couldn't leave her now, couldn't make that choice, except he'd come back just for his family. Seraphina wasn't yet part of his family. The people of Blessings had to see her for who she was. For most, she was probably little more than a story, not even truly real.

"Seraphina is too frightened of anyone who takes too much notice of her," Cort said. "I tried to get her to talk, but she was plum scared. I can't get her to come out and face people. I wasn't even willing to do that for a long time. We all have a face we put on, things we're hiding from. Every last one of us. Admitting who we are takes more guts than most have."

He'd need the strength of two, not only to portray who he really was to the town, but to stand beside Seraphina as she did.

"I think, until you've convinced your family that you want to build that trust, and work toward actually building it with the whole town, you'd best stay far from the woods. We'll go back to watching over Seraphina."

Though the truth looked him right in the face, choosing it was a physical ache. In order to do what he'd come back to Blessings for, he'd have to walk away from Seraphina for a time, just as her brother had.

AFTER TAKING a few hours to clean up the mess left by the earthquake and taking stock of the tinctures she had left, Seraphina sat in her rocker, at peace. She picked up her Bible and ran her finger down the worn spine. So often, she'd turned to the book as more of a companion than just a guide. It was a solace for her in her grief. For when everyone else left her behind, the Word did not.

She flipped to her favorite verse, the book naturally scored there with how often she'd read and reread the passage, Psalms 27:1 *The Lord is my light and my salvation; whom shall I fear? The Lord is the strength of my life; of whom shall I be afraid?*

She'd taken so much comfort from the first part of the verse. If the Lord was her light, she didn't need any other, not the sun or anyone else. Yet, the second part continued to beg for her attention. She'd wanted to throw off her fear, but it was too heavy, too full of pain. Too fraught with danger.

Now Geoff was there, expectant and calling her to a life she'd never known. He'd asked her to face her fears, for him. He'd asked of her what the Lord had been prodding for many years. The fear was still very real, but now she wanted to face it. There was a reason. If she faced the town of Blessings, she could work and live alongside Geoff. He might even love her someday. A giddy warmth spread over her chest. It was difficult to even imagine love, when her life had been so devoid of it.

She hadn't asked him before he'd departed when she should go to the livery to visit him, but if the Lord had been showing her all this time that she should, and had provided Geoff to guide her, she could do what she'd never done before.

He would be the busiest in the morning, but if she waited until the afternoon, there would be people there. Neither was convenient. If she arrived when he couldn't see her, Cort might wonder why she was there. Arrive too late, and someone from town might confront her.

It would be best to wait until between the noon meal and early afternoon, but the sun would be at its peak then. She risked a severe burn if the wind blew her hood off or if she were jostled in the street. Though she could prevent as much as possible by holding the hood in place, that seemed to scare people even more than just wearing the garment.

The little blue bottle Geoff had purchased for her the first day he'd come sat on her table. She'd rescued it from the floor while cleaning up the broken glass and mess. It was one of the few bottles that hadn't been damaged. The smooth cool surface calmed her. Martin had given her a similar bottle with cold water in it to put under her thin blanket while staying with the doctor in Coloma.

When they'd stayed there, Martin had looked at her as he patted her hand. "Don't you want to know more about that medicine they're working on?"

She was so weak, it was too much of a strain to even think about travel. "I just want to be better, Martin. How much farther until we can stop?" She'd hoped he would agree to stay there, since the doctor already knew and accepted them. Leaving to find some treatment wasn't possible. Her brother had been called to the mountains by an ad in the paper. Miners were needed in a little town named Blessings and Martin had been sure that was the place they could finally find peace.

He had, and she'd found a prison.

"Oh, Martin. What did I do to send you away? Why didn't you at least tell me?" The bottle lost its calming effect and she set it back on the table. Would she fear every person who came into her life would leave?

The hour passed and she ignored her earlier decision to go after lunch. The day made her sleepy the longer she was awake and her eyelids drooped. She rested her head on her shoulder for only a moment and startled awake at the sounds of clanging outside. Women and men talked nearby as they cooked their supper outside, avoiding the heat indoors.

It was late, but not yet evening. Geoff should've finished his day and come back home. He'd said he would, yet he wasn't there. Had he changed his mind when she didn't come as she'd said? Seraphina donned her cape and gloves, not wanting him to think she'd forgotten him.

She hid deep in her cloak as she left her house. All noise stopped as people turned to stare. She made a quick glance around at the various little houses, then made her way to the trail leading down the hill and into town. No one stopped her, but she could feel the heat of their eyes on her.

The livery was a long walk from her cabin and once she was down the hill and into town, most of the area was cleared of trees and there was no shade to hide in. Her cloak became unbearably hot within minutes. She couldn't fan her face or she might risk her hood falling out of place.

Once she was close enough to see Geoff and Cort working at the livery, her heart calmed just a bit and she slowed her steps. The man she'd thought was Cort was actually someone she didn't know and she slowed even more. She'd hoped to avoid people if she could. Perhaps at some point she would be ready to meet people, but this was just a visit to see Geoff.

She approached slowly and the man glared at her in annoyance. Geoff took a moment to glance at her, then back to the man he'd been helping.

"You that woman on the hill, ain't you?" He spat a large wad of tobacco over the fence.

There were many women that lived on the hill, but she'd been there the longest. "Yes, I live up near the river." She purposely kept her voice low, but tried to keep the timidity out of it as much as possible.

He offered a *harrumph*, then turned his attention back to Geoff. "I don't think Atherton should allow strange women to live here. People who don't contribute to the town in any way. Don't work in the mine, don't work at all. Strange folk. Aught to leave."

Geoff shifted on his feet and glanced over his shoulder at the livery, then back to the man. "I'm sure everyone helps in any way they can."

He wasn't defending her, not really. He was diverting attention and it hurt. She'd risked her health to come out as he'd asked her to, but he wasn't willing to risk anything for her.

"I think I'll go talk to Atherton about it straight away. If we allow too many people to just take up plots, then there won't be enough land for folks who do want to work." He pounded his fist on the top rung of the fence.

Geoff glanced at her for a minute and something that looked far too much like anger lit his honey-gold eyes. "Why don't you git before something happens?" He pointed back toward the hill.

Git. Just like he would tell a wandering dog. Seraphina's heart cracked as she turned and rushed back toward the cover of the trees.

CHAPTER 19

The brief, stark pain in her eyes right before Seraphina took off hit him like a slap. He couldn't have Cort and Victor's customers scared off while he was there, but he hadn't intended to hurt her. He'd just needed her to get gone before Mr. Aimes went further than just hinting at what he would do. Though, Atherton was more likely to take the man down a peg without Aimes ever realizing it had happened.

Aimes was already halfway down the street, headed to Main, probably to find Atherton at his office. If she riled up the town just by venturing outside, then he'd best let her just stay there until he could build some trust, just as Cort had suggested. Had he been away from society for so long he'd forgotten how it worked?

When he had that trust built, he'd do what Lenora and Cort should've done—use the new trust they had in him then bring her in. If they trusted him, they might believe what he had to say about her. But that wouldn't work if he didn't earn it first.

Victor strode to the gate and leaned on the fence. His usually smug face was placid, meaning he was either hiding his feelings like he did when he played cards, or he really felt nothing. "How's she doing?"

There was only one *she* they had discussed other than Lenora and Victor wouldn't need to ask about her.

"Why do you want to know?" Had he witnessed the scene with Aimes? If he had, Victor could easily fire him for inviting the woman who would scare his customers away. Victor hadn't wanted him there to begin with and would be looking for a good reason to get rid of Geoff.

"I was worried." He glanced off up the hill, avoiding Geoff's eyes. "My wife cares about her. Lenora doesn't cry often, but when she came home, she cried in my arms over that woman. Now, I know some of that is from her condition. She flies off the handle easily these days."

Geoff had to agree there. He'd picked a mighty precarious time to be returning. "So you care about Seraphina's well-being because your wife does?" It just proved that his plan was sound. If the town cared about him, they would be more likely to listen.

"I didn't say I *cared* about her. I was worried. If that woman gets better, then my wife won't worry so much."

Gripping the railing tightly, he controlled his fists. Punching Victor square in the jaw might feel good, but it would hurt his cause. "Might not kill you to actually care."

Victor leaned closer to the fence. "I know you think

you can convince everyone that you're back, a changed man. That you aren't the man who left Lenora to deal with the aftermath of her mother jumping off their home, but I know better. You forget, I've gone through a change like that. The people here won't readily forget. I won't readily forget. You are the same selfish child who left five years ago."

It *could've* been because Victor had done a measure of changing on his own, but he couldn't see into Geoff's soul. He still didn't want to take after his father, but didn't his desire to help Seraphina prove he wasn't as selfish as he'd been before?

"You don't know me. You haven't even tried. You don't know why I'm here. My family is my whole motivation. I wouldn't even be here if not for them."

Victor laughed. "Your whole motivation? Your father has sat up there alone since you got here. You've visited him once?"

Geoff turned away to keep Victor from his victory. It was true. He'd come home to make amends, yet all he'd done was build a bridge right to Seraphina. He'd only forced himself to face Lenora because of her. He'd only gone back to his father's house for clothes, not the meal his father had invited him to. He'd failed. He'd put Seraphina above his own reasons for returning. Every time he faced a new situation, he changed his mind about her. Every time he saw her, he was drawn back into her. For that reason, he needed to stay the course, and stay away from the beguiling Seraphina.

GIT.

He'd told her to git. Seraphina made it to the edge of the trees and rounded a nice big one for protection from the sun, and from view. Geoff shaded his eyes and stared her way, but she stayed hidden behind the tree. He'd asked her to come, then had stayed at work beyond his scheduled time, avoiding her. Instead of welcoming her and telling her why he was late, he'd instead listened to the strange, threatening man and told her to leave.

If she dodged through people, she might be able to make it to Lenora's. One last glance at Geoff and she discovered he was distracted by Victor. With Lenora's husband occupied, she could visit without worry. She owed Lenora gratitude for cleaning and bandaging her wound and she was already out. If Geoff did come after her, she didn't want him to find her back at her cabin. He would never suspect she'd gone to Lenora's. She waited until there were less people in the street and all who had seen her had dispersed. The heat bore down on her and the inside of her cloak was like an oven.

She made a dash for Lenora's. About halfway between the tree she'd used as a hiding place and Lenora's front door, Geoff caught sight of her and called her name. She turned for only a moment, but caught sight of him. He'd sent her away and she wouldn't go back there. People turned to stare as she quickened her pace. Only a block to go. A few people stared, open mouthed, pointing at her. Seraphina tugged her head deeper into her hood, but the heat of the sun was nothing compared to their glares.

A boy, no more than twelve, ran up to her. He snickered in her face as he danced around her. She tried to dodge around him, but he spread his arms wide. "Who's afraid of the mean ol' witch?"

Geoff called again, but she refused to take her eyes off the boy. What if he tried to take her cape? She backed away a step and he raced around behind her, laughing and taunting.

Tears stung her eyes as she searched the growing crowd for a friendly face, but found none. Only curiosity or uncertainty. In the little town that had been so accepting of everyone, she found no friend. The boy raced around her one last time, then shoved her to the ground. She landed hard and her hood flew off.

Everyone around gasped at the site of her. She groped for the hood, but it had twisted during her fall and she couldn't pull it up. Geoff landed on the ground next to her, his hands at her neck in a moment as he yanked the hood back up.

He glared at the boy as he jumped to his feet. "What's wrong with you? Why would you do such a thing? Has she ever done anything to you? No, she's probably helped you without your parents ever telling you. She's made medicines for many of you. Have you ever bothered to help her as much as she's tried to help you? Did you ever give her anything in return besides strife?"

She didn't recognize anyone in the street as long-time

members of Blessings, but she did recognize some of them as people who had come for salves and cold remedies. Her skin prickled and burned. Her face boiled to life and she hid behind Geoff. He'd been help she hadn't expected.

Geoff took her hand and led her the rest of the way to Lenora's, but he didn't say another word. He held her hand tightly in his own, and she could feel the anger coursing through him even through her gloves. Lenora opened the door before they reached the stoop and motioned them inside.

"Geoff, go to the galley and get some milk out of storage. Hurry." Lenora carefully pulled back Seraphina's hood and gave her an appraising look. "I'm thankful you explained to me what to do in case you were ever burned so badly you couldn't help yourself, or I wouldn't know what to do. It isn't bad yet. You were in the sun for less than a minute. Hopefully I can stop the burn before it gets a head start."

Geoff rushed out of the room toward the back. Lenora watched him for a moment, then tugged Seraphina to the back corner of the room. She went to the windows and drew the curtains closed, then finally sat on an ottoman facing Seraphina. There were so many hurts between them, words wouldn't come.

"You believe me now?"

Lenora closed her eyes and bowed her head. "You must understand. I did believe, even though it was hard. I had no way to even imagine what you might go through. I'm sorry."

Seraphina wanted to tell her she needn't worry, but having a friend who didn't believe her word until she was shown evidence was painful.

"Why?" Lenora gently touched Seraphina's forehead, then pulled up slightly and stared at the skin above her eye.

"Geoff asked me to." Though, he'd asked her to come to the livery, she'd chosen to go to Lenora's all on her own.

"That fool is going to get you hurt."

He already had, but he'd also been the one to help her. She'd been at once tossed aside and yanked back. Geoff had done a lot of that with her.

"He is no fool." Her heart wanted to see him return, defend himself. She wanted to see his eyes land on her marred skin and not be repulsed. Yet she couldn't quite bring herself to hope.

"You're right, of course. It's easy to hold onto that anger, but he left years ago. And I'd be lying if I didn't say that there were times I wished I could leave too."

Seraphina unhooked the clasp on her cape and removed it, then slowly pulled off her gloves. At least they had kept her arms safe. Her face would be itchy and mottled with blisters for a few weeks, but at least she could still work. Lenora took the garment and hung it by the door.

"It should've been me, out there defending you," Lenora said. "I've done just that with my husband. Atherton, though he'd never met you until recently, has done that with miners who complained about you. Pati has raved about your salve to the washerwomen. If we all came together at once and defended you, this treatment wouldn't stand. But it takes many at once."

That was why her brother had never bothered. Nothing he could say to anyone would make a difference, especially when just looking at her proved she was just as strange as they assumed.

"Don't bother," Seraphina said. "I've decided there is no reason for me to stay in Blessings. I'll go back to my house until they forget about me, then I've decided to go back to France."

"No!"

Seraphina and Lenora both turned to find Geoff in the doorway, holding a glass bottle of milk.

"I was wondering what was keeping you." Lenora reached for it. "Now, go get me a clean rag so I can put this on her face."

"No." He stood, glaring down at his sister. "You go get it. I need to talk to Seraphina."

His promises and words meant nothing. He'd told her he would stay, but hadn't. He'd told her he would come, then didn't. He told her to visit, then sent her away. Her heart wanted to trust his words, but her mind could not and she would not let his words sway her now.

Seraphina held up her hand for silence, then drew a long trembling breath. Her face still felt as if it were burning, even minutes after she'd been removed from the sunlight. "No more talking, Geoff. You've made your choice. Thank you for coming to my rescue, but you need not concern yourself with me anymore."

CHAPTER 20

Lenora returned with cloths to use as compresses, interrupting whatever Geoff would've said. Seraphina told herself no matter what he'd planned to say, he'd proven his heart in his actions. He'd left her, just as her brother had. Geoff had come back to Blessings for Lenora, not her.

A stiff silence built between brother and sister as he moved from his spot to give Lenora room. She laid the rags in her lap and took up the milk with a heavy sigh. "This may hurt or it may sooth, I don't know. I've never burned so badly."

If they had been back at her cabin, she would've suggested a salve of plantain leaves, but the milk would cool her skin and stop the reaction. It wouldn't stop the itch, though. Seraphina reached for her face and Geoff scrambled to grab her wrists. His brows rose slightly and concern rippled across his face.

"Don't. It's not that bad right now, but you could

make it worse. Lenora, go on." He held her hands firmly in his own and stared at her.

She wanted to cover her face, duck away from his gaze, but he held her fast, keeping her from moving. Lenora dampened the cloths with milk and used them as a compress, finally asking Geoff to help Seraphina lay back so the cloth could lay on her face and do the most good to cool the inflamed skin. He continued to hold her hands and she was glad of the cover of the cloth, protecting her from his gaze, and him from seeing the ugly burn.

"Are you going to just sit there or finally tell me why you're here?" Lenora asked. "We had just started getting along fine without you, then you had to come back." A rustling announced Lenora was now on her feet and moving, but Geoff continued to hold Seraphina's hand, the pressure increasing ever so slightly.

"I came back for a few reasons. First, because something happened that made me see I needed family more than anything else. Family, my blood kin, are the only ones who will ever really understand me, know where I come from, and where I belong. Secondly, I came back because *Maman's* voice wouldn't let me abandon the family any longer." His thumb traced a circle around the sensitive skin on the underside of her wrist, and Seraphina held her breath just as she tried to control all of the fluttery feelings the action loosed.

Lenora's silence left Seraphina aching to jump in, help, ask questions, and force the two to continue talking. If only she could do that with her own brother. If he ever came back, she wouldn't ever allow anger to come between them, if she could help it. He'd done so much for her and she'd always taken it for granted that he would be there.

"Where you belong? It took you five years to realize you didn't belong in brothel after brothel, playing cards and living off whiskey? Five years you could've been here, working, learning a trade. If you didn't want to be a lawyer, you should've just told father. Instead, you ran off like a coward."

Seraphina flinched at the word and Geoff stroked her hand with his. "I was. I admit it. I had to face near-death before I realized I *was* a fool and a coward. But I'm back, doesn't that mean anything? I ask your forgiveness, Lenora. Father has asked me to stay, but I won't if you don't want me here. I won't make him choose between us."

Lenora ignored his plea. "Almost died? Did you drink yourself into a stupor? Some card sharp get the better of you? How do you *almost* die in a whore house?"

Seraphina didn't know Geoff's history, but like her, he shouldn't be forced to tell it under duress. She sat up and the cloth fell off her face. She tugged her hand free of Geoff and swiped at the milk running down her cheeks. Her hands quivered and she clutched them to get her emotions under control.

"Stop. Stop, both of you. Don't you realize what you have? The gift you've been given? Lenora, he's come back. The brother you thought you would never see again has returned. My brother disappeared and has never come back, never sent a letter. I have no idea where he's gone. Pati's father had disappeared for so long and she searched for him. She could remind you how wonderful it is to have someone you love return to you. Don't you see the blessing?"

Seraphina turned to Geoff. He sat in silence, the mouth that usually smiled at her now held a firm line. Would he understand she was defending him? Would he accept defense from her? "Geoff, you must understand Lenora's hurt. You can't just leave because she doesn't open her heart back up to you right away. She was there, with your mother, the day she died. It's a deep scar."

Lenora's face relaxed and turned away, her shoulders falling.

"You have no idea how deep that scar is. It took me a year not to cry every single day. Then I dealt with the guilt. My own guilt, for wishing for freedom from her while she was alive. You weren't here. You were off avoiding life while I was forced to take on more. Just like at Father's law office, you got what you wanted and I was left with the spoils."

Geoff stood and braced his hands at his sides. "No, I wasn't. I didn't see all that you did. I wasn't there for you before I left, either. I've asked for forgiveness, I can't go back and make a different choice. I don't even think you'd really want me to. You remember how I was. I was a man who would've been more of a burden than a help."

Lenora waved her hand slightly, as if his words were of no consequence. "As I said while you were out of the room. I would be lying if I didn't admit I wished at times I could leave too, run away like you did. The last few years have been hard, even with Victor's help. Victor loves me, but nothing can heal the wound of watching your mother choose freedom in death over a life with you. I walked around for months without allowing myself to feel anything where anyone might see me. In the quiet of my home, I allowed myself to hurt. Victor knew. Father needed more and more help and that fell to us, so I blamed the only person who couldn't defend himself." She glanced over her shoulder at Geoff. "You."

Geoff went to Lenora. "I'm sorry for that. I wish I could go back and fix it, but I can't. I wasn't anywhere near a man back then. I firmly believe you would've wished I'd left."

"A man doesn't run, Geoff. This town won't be free of trouble and it's been stirred up today. And are you a man now? Will you stay? Will you stand by Seraphina and the mess you kicked up?" Lenora wrapped her arms about her waist.

"Yes, I am. I'm ready to start a business, maybe even think about a family." He glanced over at Seraphina and she averted her eyes, but she could feel the heat of his gaze, even without seeing it. Family was important to Geoff, he shouldn't be looking at her, she wasn't important to him. He'd proven it when he'd told her to git, when he hadn't kept his word to return, when he'd left her before the earthquake. No matter how much she wanted to be, she would never be loved by him.

Victor strode in the front door, his glance flitting to each person in the room. "Well, isn't this just a happy little reunion? You've certainly got the town worked into a froth. Atherton came over to the livery to let me know I should head on home and make sure all was well. He dealt with Aimes." Victor went to Lenora and slid an arm around her waist. He whispered something in her ear and she smiled.

"It's fine, Victor. He's apologized, and he's here to make it right."

"And what of her?" His frosty stare left Seraphina exposed and she turned to the wall to hide her face.

"We've talked about Seraphina before, Victor. You have nothing to fear. She is a God-fearing woman who has a skin ailment that forces her to stay indoors. You saw what happened when she came out today. It is reactions like yours that keep her from becoming a part of this town, even more than the sun."

Geoff's scent reached her just before his comforting hands rested on her shoulders. "Atherton doesn't want you to go. You know Pati, Cort and Hannah Nelson, the doctor, and so many others from Blessings. The people who have lived here the longest, accept you. It's those people who live for the mines, who come and go, who listen to gossip and superstition, who believe the lies. Come out, Seraphina. Don't stay hidden any longer."

She rested her hand over his, but she couldn't listen. He'd encouraged her to come out before, and he'd chosen those very people over her.

"I think it's time I went back home, and packed for my trip."

CHAPTER 21

Geoff stared after Seraphina as she whipped on her cloak and stuffed her fingers into her long gloves. If he left with her, he may never get another chance to talk with Lenora. If he stayed with Lenora, Seraphina may leave and he might never find her again.

Lenora patted Victor's hand, then glided across the room. "Geoff, you look like she just struck you over the head with a leaded glass pitcher. Whether we mend our ways or not, you're here. If you want to stay here, I suggest you follow her and stop listening to everyone else. I know you're afraid to listen to your heart, because it sent you in the wrong direction years ago, but one false step doesn't mean you should never trust your judgement again."

He took a deep breath. "We aren't finished, are we? I want to talk more."

Lenora glanced back to Victor for a moment and

waited for his nod, then smiled. "No, we aren't finished. Family supper with Father is Saturday. You may bring whomever you'd like."

Geoff laughed for a moment, then dashed for the door. "Thank you, I won't miss it." He ran outside and down the street. Seraphina's caped figure dodged behind the trees at the edge of Blessings. If he called after her, everyone would turn and stare. She didn't need to be the center of any more attention that day.

He raced after her, his heart pumping and feet stumbling. The town never seemed so long. When he reached the tree line, he slowed down and tried to avoid the little homesteads that dotted the wooded landscape. He couldn't see Seraphina or her red cape any longer, but he knew the way to her cabin.

He reached her house and waited by the door as he caught his breath. If he couldn't talk with her, then he couldn't convince her of his regret, and that he spent too much time listening to others and not his heart. But *had* he listened to his heart, really listened? He closed his eyes and leaned against the wall of her cabin. Her slight smile was unforgettable, the lilt of her voice as she spoke in French, and tried to speak in English. The way she cared for others even when she was terrified they'd label her a witch marked her for the generous person she was.

How had he not seen it? His heart had chosen her.

Geoff knocked lightly on her door, waited for a moment, then opened it slightly. Seraphina gasped and dashed her hood back up, hiding from the light.

"Is that how people come to see you and get

convinced you aren't here? You don't answer?" His heart warmed and throbbed at the sight of her, even with her pink cheeks from the burn, she was the loveliest woman he'd ever seen.

"I was going to lay down. I only slept for a few hours today so I didn't answer. This is when I usually sleep and I certainly didn't expect you to follow me." She turned from him and removed her cape then hung it up near the stove.

"I know, you didn't sleep because I asked you to come to see me. I got scared when your visit didn't go like I thought it would. I'm so sorry, Seraphina. Can you forgive me? I've been giving a lot of apologies lately. I'm nowhere near perfect, but I'm trying to be better."

Her hands rested on her cloak, as if she might change her mind and whip it back on so she could run. "I waited for you, all day. You said you would come back, but it got to be supper and you didn't so I went to find you."

"If it had been one of the people you know and not Aimes when you came—" He could only speculate. Even people who liked Seraphina for her medicines might have thought it strange to find her out by the livery in broad daylight when they'd never seen her out before. "I should've had you come to church with me first."

Seraphina sobbed on a humorless laugh. "You think church would save me from their words, their thoughts? They hate me. Aimes was just willing to say it." Her shoulders shuddered and he wanted to go to her but held back. He couldn't say why, but he knew if he touched her just then, he would lose her.

"You're hurt because of me. Don't place your anger with anyone but me. You have every right to be hurt, but I'm the one who hurt you, not them. I'm the one who owes you not only an apology, but a thank you."

Her head swung around to stare at him and her golden cat eyes caught him off-guard with their brightness. "Thank you? What have I possibly done to earn that?"

He took a deep breath and collected his words. If he said the wrong thing now, he might drive her away. "Without you, I would never have been able to speak to Lenora. I would never have known she also saw her insecurities as a block between us. It wasn't just me. If you hadn't defended me, spoken up, we would've continued to fight and Victor would've come home to raised voices. I would've been tossed out on my ear."

She clutched her hands together in a tight grip. "I only wanted you to see what you refused to. You both were looking through a lens clouded by the past and your own anger. You came back. My brother didn't and never will. You have a chance so many won't."

"I know, and she sees that now. It's all thanks to you." He reached for her fingers and squeezed them. She tried to pull away from him, but with little effort. They were both trapped by the skin they'd been given. But could they both find a new life in Blessings if they would only step out of the shadows?

"Seraphina..." He had to show her what he'd hoped to keep from everyone. He had to bare his soul just as she'd bared hers to build trust where he'd destroyed it.

Only then could they know each other and bear the burden. "I need you to see this, to understand me better. It might help you to see that I'm not so different from you."

He let go of her hands and unbuttoned the cuffs of his sleeves, held in his breath and prayed she would understand and not see only his gruesome scars, but him, the man who was growing to care for her so much he ached with it. He rolled the sleeves up to his elbows and held out his arms for her to see, turning them slowly to show both the back and front. "I told you that a man tried to change my skin, and found it impossible." Though the scarring did make him lighter in areas, he was still much darker than her.

She gasped. "Oh, Geoff." Even gloved, her fingers tenderly ran up his arm. Miss Rosa had been kind and gentle, but had left him unmoved. When Seraphina touched him, his pulse raced and his mouth went dry.

She tugged off her gloves and led him to the lamp at the table. He allowed her to push him into the chair, then she knelt in front of him. Her practiced, clinical eye traced every line left behind by the cruel whip.

"How bad is it?" Her gaze traveled up his arm and to his face, then she flinched. "He didn't just do this to your arms, did he?" Her hesitation was laced with hope, but was it hope that she wouldn't have to look at the maze that mapped his body, or hope that he hadn't had to endure it?

He hadn't embraced anyone, or let anyone touch him without at least a coat between them for fear they would feel the bumps under his shirt. Geoff gently lifted her hand from his arm and raised it to his shoulder as she stood to reach. She gasped as her fingers probed alongside his undershirt against the raised skin there. She let her hand wander down his back and she carefully examined him through his shirt all the way down to the waistband of his trousers.

"We are the same, Seraphina. Trapped by our skin. But maybe it matters less than we think. Maybe, together, we can find the happiness that has been impossible until now because the people who love us are here?" He stood and turned to face her. Her eyes were wide, willing. He stepped closer and tenderly took her face in his hands. She didn't pull away. Her cheeks were slightly rough from the burn, but he wanted to hold her, let her know the same way her touch had told him—she was worthy, beautiful.

She flushed pink and tried to tip her face away from him, but her hands held his waist. Her hold told him without her having to say a word that she didn't want him to leave. She was so used to shying away from people that she wouldn't look him in the eye. They could teach each other the best way, if she would let him. He leaned in, wanting her full acceptance of him, needing to know she desired him even after what he'd shown her and what he'd done.

She turned her face slightly at the last moment and, instead of capturing her lips as he'd hoped, he kissed her cheek. He held her close, praying his heart beat loudly in her ear so she would know just how she affected him. She was so tiny in his arms, so fragile, but finally he held her. He let his mouth roam over her temple, her ear, then the top of her head, and she held his shirt tighter, pulling him near. If she wasn't ready to kiss him, at least she didn't push him away.

"You haven't told me if you accept my apology," he whispered into her hair as he wrapped his arms around her tighter, memorizing the feel of her there, clutched close, protected.

"*Oui*," the word escaped on a breath. "Yes, fool that I am, I do." She stepped back to look him in the eyes. "I don't know what you plan, to make everyone believe I mean them no harm, but I trust you."

Her words filled him. He hadn't realized how much he'd needed to hear them from someone. He'd striven to be a man in everyone's eyes for so long, but it was trust, the one thing he'd lacked, that was the last piece to the puzzle.

"I'll find a way. I refuse to force you to hide here a moment longer. You have so much to offer." He reached for her face once more and she shied away.

"No. Please don't. It's so ugly." She tried to step back, out of his embrace.

"To you? Perhaps. To me, no. Most certainly, no."

While he wanted to stay right there with Seraphina, he couldn't. Not with the sudden full realization of his desire for her. She would want him to stay, but he would do this the right way, the way his *Maman* would want him to. She'd guided him correctly so far. He would stay at the livery one more night, but tomorrow would be a new day.

"Come with me to family supper tomorrow?" He prayed she would, even after her disastrous time that day.

"At Lenora's?" Her face fell slightly.

"Yes, Father will be there." It would be the perfect place to convince his father that Seraphina was no different than anyone else.

"I will go, for you." Her lips curved in a slight smile.

"Then I will see you tomorrow evening." He kissed her temple once more and held her close. She clung to him for a moment and he hated letting her go. Hopefully soon, with a little help from others and if she felt as he did, he wouldn't have to.

CHAPTER 22

The room didn't seem quite so small anymore. Seraphina glanced around her little cabin and smiled. The spot where she and Geoff had embraced still held a bit of inner warmth. She'd never been held so tenderly, and his kiss, she sighed as she thought about his lips on her face. If a kiss on the cheek felt so wonderful, a kiss on the lips would surely make her burst.

She'd planned to lay down, even though it was evening and when she normally was starting her day, but her mind was too active to think about rest now. Resting had been her plan when she'd thought Geoff and Lenora would keep fighting until he left, and when she'd thought he could never share her love, because he'd been embarrassed by her. He'd only been unsure. That could be forgiven, and she had.

Someone knocked on her door and she turned her back to it. "Please, enter." Before today, she wouldn't have allowed anyone to come in without first knowing who it was, but today she'd realized her love for Geoff, and he loved her in return.

"Afternoon." The slow drawl of Mr. Winslet came from the doorway.

She turned slightly to see him standing in the light, only holding the door open a little. "Do come in and close it behind you." She pulled out the chair next to her at the table and went to the stove to put on some coffee.

"Thank you." He softly closed them in and ambled inside, seating himself where she'd indicated. "I keep a good eye on most folks in my little town, and I've watched you as best I could. Seems like right about now is the time when I might be able to help you the most."

It was rude to keep her back to a guest, but her face was still bumpy from the sun, and probably red, not to mention the jagged gash on the side of her face. She hated turning to look at him. "I will be thankful for any help you can offer." She slowed her speech and made sure every word was the right one before she spoke it. Geoff understood most of her French, but most in Blessings wouldn't.

"Your brother sent a letter from Virginia."

That was where the doctor had said they had been researching cures for her sun disease. Her heart quickened. "Martin...sent you a letter?" Her hand shook and she gripped the short dry sink next to her stove for support. Three years was a long time. She'd thought he was dead, or just didn't care. Could it really be him?

"Yes. Not only did he find one of your aunts, he

found a possible treatment for you. But he can't leave your aunt Annalise. She has fallen on hard times and Martin is helpin' her."

Suddenly Seraphina was faced with a life-changing choice: leave Blessings for a possible treatment and see her brother again, or stay with Geoff and his family. When he'd sat by her bed so long ago, asking about the possibility of finding a cure, it had been because he cared. He'd left because of her, not to get away from her. "Did he say anything else?"

Atherton cleared his throat and she remembered she hadn't given him his coffee yet. She poured a cup and set it in front of him, then sat down.

He nodded his thanks and took a bracing sip. "He didn't." He drew the letter out of his pocket and handed it to her. "He sent it to me because he wasn't sure if you'd stayed on. If I might give my own advice?" He raised his white eyebrows and waited for her response.

"Go ahead." She needed some sort of guidance. While it was tempting to run off after Martin because she had missed him, she had very little money and travel would be difficult at night, especially alone.

"To my way of thinkin', until they can be sure that treatment works, you should stay here. Don't pay no mind to Aimes or anyone like him. There're too many good folks in Blessin's who would be happy to see you. One especially." He laughed and took another sip.

"One?" Who could he know who would be happy to see her?

"One of the Farnsworths, I think."

It was her turn to laugh and she found she liked it. She hadn't had much to laugh about in a very long time. She didn't understand how the old man knew about Geoff, when she'd barely found out herself that he cared, but it mattered little.

"I truly don't know what to do. I miss my brother and care about him, but I can't leave. Not now. If I'd gotten the message even a day ago—" She bit off her words. Even if she'd heard them a few hours before, she would've been making plans to leave.

"I also came to tell you, the preacher has decided to do a candlelight service this Sunday. Thought it would be right pretty. It starts at eight, when the sun has set for the night." He stood and tugged on his suspenders. "Might be a good time to meet some old friends." He nodded and touched his hat, then turned and let himself out.

If Geoff's father accepted her, then she would join Geoff and attend the little church for the first time. She stared down at the letter and picked it up. The address on it was in her brother's stilted letters. She couldn't go, not all the way to Virginia. Not without someone to go with her. She would write to Martin and let him know. If the doctors ever did find a cure, she would ask Geoff to take her, but until then, Blessings was home.

GEOFF LED Seraphina down the hill toward Blessings.

181

Though she was covered in her cape, to protect her from the evening summer sun and to hide the remnants of her burn, no one approached them this time. In fact, many people tipped their hat in his direction. After the first few, he'd realized he wasn't imagining it. The town was giving them a silent welcome. He smiled and nodded back to each one.

He knocked on Victor and Lenora's door and his father answered. He smiled as he laid eyes on Geoff, then opened the door wide to let them in. "Geoff, so good to see you." He hurried to close the door and Victor came in. He smiled slightly at Seraphina and closed the drapes, cutting the evening sun from the room.

Geoff helped Seraphina out of her cape as she sent a narrow-eyed glance around the room. He could understand her skepticism. She'd encountered nothing but fear until then.

His father stood, hands clasped and relaxed. "Geoff, will you introduce your guest?"

He drew Seraphina closer and held her small waist. She was lovely in a pale gold dress. He'd never seen her in anything but black and red. When he'd arrived to take her to supper, she'd surprised him by not only wearing a dress other than black, she'd put her black hair up in a coil around her head. She was so lovely, he couldn't look away.

"Father, this is Miss Seraphina Beaumont, my guest for the evening."

He nodded his acceptance and approached her,

holding out his hand. When she placed her hand in his, he kissed her knuckles lightly. "Good evening, a pleasure to meet you, Miss Beaumont. I'm Edward Farnsworth. Welcome."

Victor led them back to the dining room and stood by his place. Lenora had left elegant place cards by each seat and had assumed he'd bring a guest. He pulled out the seat next to his and Seraphina sat. Lenora brought in a large roast with assorted vegetables and Victor rushed to take the heavy platter from her and moved it to the table.

Lenora smiled her welcome and Victor seated her, then Edward and Victor sat at either end of the table. Edward led the table in grace, then Victor sliced the roast and served everyone at the table.

Father ate a few bites then glanced at him. "Lenora tells me you've considered staying on in Blessings, perhaps starting a business?" He paused, his face expectant.

"Yes. I'd noticed that Blessings is a growing town, but there's nowhere to buy boots. I'm planning to go to Coloma, see if I can study with someone there to learn how it's done, then come back here and set up shop. Seraphina said she would help me." He smiled at his guest. If he found reasons to bring her into the conversation, it might draw her out. She'd said nary a word since they'd left her cabin.

"That's a good plan," his father surprised him by saying. "That building on Main would be the perfect spot, not too big. A good place to start."

He'd expected his father to at least *try* to get him to take over the family business. It wasn't as if he had no training at all. To have him encourage something new was unheard of. "I hadn't thought about a storefront yet, but yes. It would be."

His father sat back slightly and continued, "That would be a good business. Ed has to buy boots from San Francisco now, and after he pays for the boots and transporting them, they are so expensive he earns almost nothing for them. If he stops, Blessings has no boots. Men without boots can't work in the mines."

"Father?" Lenora drew the conversation to herself. "Geoff is here because of family. You, me, and...Mother. I think it's time we talk about her, about what she told me right before she died."

His father tensed slightly. "Nothing good can come of that, Lenora. It's not worth discussing."

"Not true." Seraphina spoke up, her head ducked and hands clasped in her lap. "Worse is not knowing. I know nothing about my family. All I have left are memories and a dagger that may have a clue to where I came from. My brother may have found some clues and my heart aches to know more, but I can't go. Knowing where you came from could help you. Share who you are. Don't be ashamed."

Lenora smiled, but Seraphina didn't raise her head to see it. "Thank you, I agree. Geoff, it isn't right that you're here to know what mother told me, and for me to keep it, especially when I didn't want to know." She set down her fork and took a deep breath, then squared her shoulders.

"Everyone suspected that Mother was from a slave family, we'd all heard the rumors at the parties. It didn't matter that she staunchly denied it, in fact, that only made them talk more. No one knew her family and she was never willing to tell people where she came from. It was only natural people would question her, since she did have the curly dark hair, and darker skin. Just like you, Geoff."

She stopped and pushed the food around on her plate for a moment. "I didn't want to know, and I didn't even believe it for a long time, because much of what she said right before she jumped—" Lenora closed her eyes tightly and a soft sob escaped her lips. "She wasn't in her right mind."

Geoff cleared his throat. If speaking about it hurt Lenora, then he wouldn't have her continue, no matter how much he wanted to know. "You don't have to go on."

She dabbed at her nose briefly and reached for Victor's hand. He took it and it held like a precious jewel. "No, I want to. I need to share the knowledge. It was true, Geoff. All of it was true. She hid it her whole life, was ashamed. It drove her mad, all the hiding, the lying. I'm not ashamed. I'm proud of my thick curly hair. I'm proud of who I am and who I've become." She rested her hand at her waist. "I'm proud to become a mother."

Geoff reached for Seraphina's hands, where she clutched them in her lap. He'd been wanting to know about his mother for so long, but he realized he'd known all along. His mother had denied it so vehemently, that had been the only thing holding back the truth. It didn't fill his need as he'd hoped it would. Something else had. He'd needed to feel like he belonged, and Seraphina had provided that, not the knowledge of why his skin was a different hue.

"I'm glad to finally know, but I've decided I don't want to seek out family who never wanted us. Mother told us her family rejected her letters after she married, so we all assumed they didn't want to see us. It may have just been that it would've given away her secret. She took that to the grave with her."

Father glanced up from his plate. He'd been so quiet during the whole conversation, but he now commanded attention. "That isn't exactly the case. I knew her parents. They didn't want Matilda to ever marry me. Once she left without their blessing, all her letters were returned, unopened. After a while, she stopped trying."

Geoff stared at his father for a moment and felt inside the door to his distant family close. *Maman* didn't push him to try. "We are all here, in Blessings, and I want to stay. That is, if you do?" He squeezed Seraphina's fingers to let her know he spoke to her. While he'd stay there just to be close to his father and sister, she was the family he needed most of all.

She raised her head slowly and glanced at him, then around the table. He needed her to stay with him, but he needed her to *want* it more. A smile briefly kissed her lips and she nodded. "I told you earlier my brother may have found a cure to my illness, he wrote me a letter. I know I could seek out my brother and aunt in Virginia, but they are the only family I have left. I have no one I'd rather be with than you, Geoff. Martin may return some day, but even if he doesn't, I won't be alone if I'm with you."

Once he convinced the town to accept Seraphina, they would never have to be alone again.

CHAPTER 23

Geoff rushed through the undergrowth along the river. Seraphina's flowers had been there when he'd been down there a few days before. They had to still be there now. He kept his eyes focused on the trail as he rushed. He'd worked all day, then gone up to the loft of the livery to clean up, but he'd never call the livery home again. Not after tonight, if she agreed...

He'd had Whit run to get Atherton early in the day and asked him if that night's church service might be used for two purposes. The man had been plum giddy about helping with Geoff's plan. He was to go around town and spread the word about the wedding. The bride alone would bring a good turnout. But Geoff had also requested that he come back and let him know if anyone wouldn't welcome the union. Seraphina had been hurt enough by her own brother by keeping her hidden away. He wouldn't hurt her further.

Atherton had reported that most in town were pleased for the wedding, but even more pleased that Seraphina was finally going to come out and join the community. It seemed many had wanted her to, but were unsure of how to ask.

Along the bank, where the river widened and slowed a bit, he found the flowers. Many people in Blessings used that area to bathe and he was glad no one was making use of it on this church night. He picked six of the flowers, a fresh one for her ear, and five for her to hold. Even though she was known for collecting plants, he couldn't think of her with any other flower.

The woods seemed emptier than usual as he walked back toward Seraphina's cabin, the one he hoped to share with her if the evening went as he'd planned. Only then did his heart race. She could say no, or walk away. He'd never really courted her, but he hoped it wasn't needed. They both knew, had known in the simple way they were comfortable with each other where they hadn't been with anyone else, that they were built to be one.

At her door, he waited for a moment to catch his breath, then knocked. She had on her cloak, with the hood drawn over her head to protect herself while she'd waited for him, but she wouldn't need it when they left for the church in a few minutes. It was already darkening enough to need a lantern. He went inside and waited for her to remove her cape and gloves. She wouldn't need to do that anymore either, because when he came home, he wouldn't have to knock.

He glanced around the small cabin and thought of

easy ways he could keep the direct sun out, but let in more air for her. Windows with glass would help, and he could build a shade awning on the outside to keep the sun out so that she wouldn't have to cover the windows until the afternoon.

"What are you planning, Geoff?" Her voice danced over his ears and he smiled as he turned to her.

"Many things, my Seraphina. Many things." He took one of the flowers and broke it with just a few inches of stem, then gently placed it behind her ear. Just the way she'd been when he'd found her. Just like then, the flower seemed to make her pale skin glow brighter.

He handed her the five remaining flowers. "These are for you, to mark a very special occasion."

She tilted her head. "Special? What have you planned? I was going to go to church with you tonight."

He couldn't let her be disappointed, she had wanted to go to church. "That is still the plan. Atherton spread the word to the whole town that you will be there. You'll be a guest of honor, everyone is excited to see you."

Along the wall, the last hint of sun disappeared on the window ledge where the cover had been pulled aside just slightly. Seraphina had risked a burn to watch for him.

He drew her close and sighed as she rested her head against his chest. "I don't want you to ever have to sit by that window and worry that I might not come for you. I don't want another sun to set when I'm not here with you."

She gasped and glanced up at him. "Geoff—?" the question died on her lips and her hand trembled.

"If you'll have me, the little church is ready to do a twilight service for us. Please say you'll join me, Seraphina. Say you'll be mine forever." He kissed her temple and waited for her to respond. She reached around him, pulling him closer.

"*Pour toujours?*"

He laughed, and wished he'd thought to ask her in French to stay with him always, because that would be special to her. "*Oui, Voulez-vous restez avec moi pour toujours?*"

She smiled, her face brightening and radiating more than he'd ever seen before. She was surely an angel, his angel, come to Earth to make him whole. He followed her as she led him to the door, then opened it. He took her hand and threaded it under his arm. He realized she had yet to answer him.

"Seraphina?" He tried to slow, but she kept walking. He didn't want her to stumble nor remind her she was walking without the cover of her cape, down the main trail that led from the hill to town. People waved or nodded and she nodded back, but said nothing.

They reached the little church and she stopped a few feet from the doors. He turned to face her and saw a gathering of people who had followed them like a parade. The women were dressed in their Sunday finery and carried baskets for a meal afterwards. The men were clean and shaved, except Atherton, who led Millie with tears in her eyes to the head of the group. Millie smiled and waived a dainty handkerchief at them.

Seraphina took his hands and held them for a moment before she raised her head and met his eyes. "Yes, Geoff. I will marry you, right here and now in the sight of God and the citizens of Blessings."

Atherton let off a whoop that started a chain of noise and cheering throughout the crowd. He'd never kissed his bride, but as all the congregation passed them to find seats for the celebration, he wanted a moment alone with the woman who would be his wife.

Victor, Lenora, and his father held behind and waited for him. His father stepped forward. "I would like to escort Miss Beaumont down the aisle, if I may?" He bowed slightly.

Seraphina smiled and glanced at him. "If you would like him to, I know he would be honored," Geoff said.

Seraphina stepped closer to him. "Yes, I would like that very much."

"Why don't you all go inside. We'll be there in just a moment."

His wedding would be short, but the length of the sermon didn't matter. Not only would he gain a bride, but a whole new outlook. Seraphina had a way of looking at life and all living things differently than other people he'd met.

"I'm nervous." She stepped closer and tucked her face into his chest. Her trust made him even more of a man, even more than all the pain he'd been through to get there.

"We have our whole lives to learn. We'll take it slow." He tipped her face up and her lips parted slightly. The moon had not yet risen, the sun had set, but he could still see her face easily in the light from the windows in the church.

He drew her lips to his and she didn't pull away or turn her face. The connection he felt to her coiled softly around him until it became a part of who he was. He could no longer tell where he ended and she began. Though he wanted to explore, to kiss her to his full content, the whole town waited for a wedding, and now there was nothing pulling him away. He could stay in Blessings and they could make each other whole for the rest of their days.

Brothers of Belle Fourche

Teach Me to Love

What the Heart Holds

Deep Longing of the Soul

Saved By Grace

When Shadows Break

Along A Tangled Path

A Lady Loves Much

Next book in the Brides of Blessings Series

Birth of the Butterfly ～ Mimi Milan

ABOUT THE AUTHOR

Kari Trumbo is an author of Christian historical and contemporary Romance and a stay-at-home mom to four vibrant children. When she isn't writing or editing, she homeschools her children and pretends to keep up with them. Kari loves reading, listening to contemporary Christian music, singing with the worship team, and curling up near the wood stove when winter hits. She makes her home in central Minnesota with her husband of over twenty years, two daughters, two sons, one cat and one hungry wood stove.

You can get a free book for signing up at www.KariTrumbo.com

Made in the USA
Monee, IL
19 August 2021